DANGEROUS JUSTICE

Sherry Joyce

Published by Hummingbird Flight Press

SHERRY JOYCE

Published by Hummingbird Flight Press

Partial proceeds from the sale of this book go to St. Jude's Hospital and The Cystic Fibrosis Foundation.

Dedication

To Jim, my husband, for his unwavering support and helpful suggestions. To my mother, Olga, who raised me to believe I could accomplish anything, even the impossible.

Other books by Sherry Joyce on Amazon.com

The Dordogne Deception
Dangerous Duplicity

Web: http://sherryjoyce.com

PROLOGUE
Nick

Nick Fontaine lounged on his sailboat, *Slipped Away*, in faded shorts with his legs crossed and a flip-flop dangling on his big toe. He dozed on and off with a beer in one hand, resting the cold bottle on his deeply tanned chest, and expanded colorful tattoo covering the bullet wound below his shoulder. Even in this relaxing environment, it was hard not to let his mind drift to his criminal past, memories that would haunt him his whole life.

He cringed when he remembered his youth—his abusive, alcoholic father and his brilliant but deranged brother, Ted, who orchestrated an unsuccessful bank robbery four years earlier in El Dorado Hills, California. How he tried to put that horrible day behind him. As the robbery unraveled, Ted accidentally shot several people, even fatally wounding the little six-year old sister of an off-duty El Dorado Hills detective, Evan Wentworth, who just happened to be in his squad car across the street from the bank. During the exchange of gunfire, Evan shot Ted in the leg. Although they both managed to escape, Ted's wound got worse. They didn't get the bullet out in time; the wound got infected and then septic. Ted died a few weeks after the robbery.

Changing his name and appearance, he made his way to Europe, where he relied on his sales management experience at a southern California boat company to become a partner at Gaspard Yachting in Nice, France. When the company's controller, Armond Fouquet, discovered he'd been embezzling funds for cocaine trafficking, he killed him before he could tell his new partner and owner of the yachting company, Gaspard DuBois.

The nightmare hadn't ended there. Unbelievably, that damn cop, Evan Wentworth had come to France on a vacation. He happened to meet Gaspard's oldest daughter, Danielle, in St. Paul-de-Vence and fell in love with her, turning what started as a vacation into a relocation to the south of France. In an attempt to evade capture during a large manhunt by the police, and Evan figured out his role in the murder and the robbery years earlier, he kidnapped Gaspard's daughter, Lena, taped her down in a raft, and sent it floating out into the ocean; he even provided its coordinates to her rescuers in order to lure Evan, her father Gaspard, and the Coast Guard out in the ocean to witness the explosion of his yacht, the *Southern Cross*, hoping they would believe he died in the blast, allowing him to escape to the island of Mallorca. Although he had survived the explosion, he deeply regretted blowing up his beautiful yacht. At least they thought he was dead.

CHAPTER ONE
Nick

Nick's unsettling reverie was shattered by the voice of his very loud neighbor.

"Hey, how's things, Nick?" His boat slip partner on his immediate west was a nice guy, but stubborn and nearly deaf. They had frequent boisterous arguments about Chad's noisy TV late at night to no avail.

"It's all good Chad, but I could sleep better if you turned down the volume at night. We've talked about this issue many times."

"Say what?" Chad cupped a hand behind his ear straining to hear.

Nick shouted. "It's your TV! I can hear it in my cabin long after midnight."

Chad frowned and staggered back and forth holding up a green bottle of Glenlivet. "Sorry, mate. I leave it on so I can fall asleep."

You're sleeping, but I can't. Please turn the damn thing down."

Chad waved a hand in the air in mock acknowledgment. "Will try to remember."

Nick, tired of this ongoing noise battle, took a deep breath. Living side-by-side in close quarters required consideration. Chad Callahan was a nice enough guy, pushing eighty, a heavy drinker, but too deaf or out cold to hear his own racket.

Chad tried to lighten the conversation. "Have any luck finding work?"

"Not yet. I'm thinking of heading up to the site of the new hotel that's being built. Maybe I can find a job."

"Doing what?" Chad balanced on the rail for support, his bushy white hair flying in his face in the breeze.

"Construction. I'm bored as hell with nothing to do all day."

"I hear it's going to be some high-flying extravaganza." Smoke wafted out of Chad's cabin. "Oh, buggers! Food's burning. Good luck. See ya'." Chad scampered into his galley.

Nick gritted his teeth and went back to struggling with thoughts about his dubious resume—embezzlement, murder rap avoided, bank robbery. Who'd hire him? What if they did a background check? He couldn't tell the truth about being a partner at Gaspard Yachting. He certainly couldn't use Gaspard as a reference. He'd have to think of some plausible skills where someone wouldn't question his background. But not today. Today was for relaxing on his boat, a necessary escape from Nice, courtesy of his drug-running submarine buddies who provided him with a passport and a new identity. The explosion ensured he was presumed dead. Newspapers printed the story. Being dead was all that mattered. Having a new life—this laidback life. No worries except making some extra money to pay for fixing the cracked boom and disgruntled engine on his boat. Boredom was unsettling, gnawing and keeping him up at night—that and Chad's

8

blaring TV. He'd not been having his usual stress migraines, but the late evening noise was pushing the limit. He rubbed his calf. The jagged scar still hurt. Shards of metal and fiberglass had flown underwater ripping away his neoprene wetsuit creating a nasty gash. The ugly scar, a constant reminder of blowing up his yacht, but being alive. If only he hadn't killed nosey Armond, the pain-in-the-ass controller who discovered his embezzlement. Big mistake. Big fucking mistake.

CHAPTER 2
Evan and Danielle

Evan stroked the side of her cheek and woke up Danielle from her nap prior to their plane landing at the Palma de Mallorca airport.

"Sleep well?"

Danielle glanced up at him. "Yes, but I'm worried?"

Evan looked at her with concern. "About what? We're supposed to have a stress-free honeymoon.

She teared up. "I miss Trevor already and we've only been gone a couple of hours. We've never left him for any length of time before. Don't you think he'll be frightened?"

"Honey, no. My mom flew in to be with your mom. What could be better than two doting grandmothers?" Evan rubbed the back of her neck to soothe her.

With pleading eyes, Danielle looked at Evan. "Promise me we'll FaceTime when we get settled."

"I promise. Stop worrying. He's a happy toddler. He'll be fine." Evan said.

The captain turned on the *fasten your seatbelts* sign."

Danielle asked. "I know you said it was a surprise, but where are we staying?"

"I wanted to treat you with something special. Do you remember my fondness for the architect Santiago Calatrava?"

Danielle squinted, pinching her forehead trying to recall the name. "I remember hearing it. Wasn't it someone you used in your final exams from Parsons?"

"Brilliant recollection. Yes, that's the architect. I found a hotel on the beach in Palma named *Calatrava*. It has a spa and a terraced café sitting on Palma's waterfront. I think you'll love it."

Danielle clapped her hands together in delight. "I can't wait. We're going to have a wonderful honeymoon vacation."

Evan shifted his seat to the upright position. "With all the stress we had in our lives after your surgery, your mom's heart surgery, and then Ryan kidnapping Lena, and—"

She scowled. "We don't talk about Ryan, ever! He's dead. Remember? Don't remind me of the traumas we survived. Promise me nothing will go wrong on our honeymoon."

Evan stroked the top of her knee. "I'm an artist now, not a cop? I've put my badge away."

CHAPTER 3
Nick and Cassandra

Nick trimmed his white-blond beard to a mere scruff, combed his hair and tied it in a bun at the nape of his neck. He put on a clean shirt and shorts, locked up his sailboat and walked the pier to his motorcycle. A day that held the promise of something new, he enjoyed a pleasant ride in cooler temperatures. He'd rehearsed his background and what he would say to the owners of the hotel.

Weaving through tunnels and past gorges open to the azure sea, the rugged coastline of the Tramuntana was breathtaking. Billowing cumulus clouds filled the sky.

He passed several cars along the road as he climbed the steep cliffs of the spectacular mountain range, but as he rode higher, it became quieter, more peaceful. He spotted the construction site in the distance, a hotel which would certainly appeal to tourists who wanted solitude instead of the busy tourist attractions of Palma.

Cranes were moving metal and lumber. Workers were framing the hotel's structure which sat on a solid foundation of concrete and bedrock. He parked his cycle, hung his helmet on the handlebars, and began the hike up to the action. Spotting a native-looking worker, he hollered above the din, "Hey there. Can you tell me who is in charge?" The man turned and pointed to a woman wearing a hardhat reviewing blueprint drawings. Nick walked to meet her.

"Excuse me. You in charge?"

"I am," she said frowning and tucking the rolled blueprints under her arm. "Cassandra Benoit. What can I do for you?" She removed her hardhat and raised her hand to shield her eyes from the sun. Jackhammers, nail guns and buzz saws created a loud din from workers assembling the framework.

He extended his hand and raised his voice. "Hi, Nick Fontaine. Looking for a job. Thought maybe you could use some construction help."

She eyed him with curiosity and raised her voice over the din. "Your timing might be great. My foreman left this morning due to a family emergency and isn't expected to return. Tell me about yourself. I'm in a rather desperate situation."

Nick stroked lose strands of hair off his forehead. He raised his voice over the noise. "I worked for my father's construction company for many years building houses, tracking shipments, keeping the books and managing the staff."

She set her hardhat on a bench. "Why are you looking for a job?"

"I live here on my sailboat and enjoy it very much, but there are only so many days I can handle doing much of nothing. I'm restless and want to work to occupy my time, and I've got some expensive boat issues that need fixing."

"Can your father vouch for you?"

He felt a rush of tension in his temples. "No, I wish. He died years ago. I didn't want to run the company and I sold it before it went under."

"Tell you what. I'll hire you on a temporary basis to see if it works out."

"Sounds great. What are your plans for the hotel?"

"Let's sit here in the shade." She pointed to an ice chest. "Do you want anything to drink?"

"A soda or a water if you have it." They sat down on a stone bench.

She handed him a bottle of water, then unfolded the building plans and showed him the blueprints. "The hotel will have one-hundred-fifty rooms, very exclusive, away from the populated areas of the island, hoping to attract wealthy patrons who want peace and solitude—a luxurious health resort."

"I'm impressed. You don't look old enough to be developing such a large project. Are you from Mallorca?"

When she smiled at him, her dark brown eyes were cautious, but warm. "I'm from Barcelona, but I'm living on the island while the project is completed. Once it's done, I intend to stay here and manage the hotel. I'm an architect and a designer.

Working on the interior design aspects is taking up most of my time. I don't want to worry about the construction issues. My father owns Benoit Construction in Barcelona and is busy with several projects there."

Nick sighed. "Seems like a lot of work. When do you plan on opening?"

"Six months from now. I want to get everything completed before the rainy season."

He cleared his throat. "How many men do you have on this project?"

"Forty now. Engineers, electricians, sheet metal workers, carpenters, plumbers—the usual."

With awe and a sincere expression, Nick asked. "What do you need most from me?"

"Avoidance of cost over-runs, tracking expenses and deliveries. Also inspecting the progress and ensuring the men do excellent work. I won't tolerate any shoddy construction."

"Understood." Nick took a swig of water and a deep breath. "When do you want me to start?"

"How's tomorrow?" She shifted the dark hair braid off her shoulder.

He laughed. "Tomorrow's good. How much are you paying?"

He watched her bite the inside of her cheek. "How's a thousand a week?"

"Sounds good." He raised his eyebrows and thought about asking for more but decided not to push it.

A cool gust of wind blew small tumbleweeds and sand across their feet. "Come see me tomorrow. I'm in the trailer on the other side of the hill. You can fill out the necessary paperwork and I'll introduce you to the crew."

He stood and extended his hand to her and flashed a charming grin. "Thanks for the job offer, Cassandra."

"My pleasure," she clasped his hand with firmness. "Call me Cassie."

"What time do you want me to start?"

"I'm usually here by 7:00, but come by at 8:00. It's when everyone else arrives."

"Sounds good. I'll see you tomorrow. Bye, Cassie."

Nick turned and walked the dirt path to his cycle, put on his helmet and began the ride down the northwestern coast. He mused to himself. That was easy—easier than he thought it would be. Seemed no need to tell her his brother, Ted, killed their alcoholic father who never worked an honest day in his life. With a new job to think about, and a gorgeous new boss, his first trip would be to the Mallorca public library to brush up on construction and local building codes for hotels. He knew how to build yachts—how complex could hotel structures be?

CHAPTER 4
Nick and Chad

The sun was setting, casting rays of glorious scarlet and auburn when Nick returned to his boat, arms full of books on hotel construction from the library. Nick saw Chad on the deck of his boat and waved hello.

Chad hollered. "Hey, Bud. That's a lot of reading. What're you doing?"

"Learning all I can about hotel construction. I landed a job." Nick set the books down on an outdoor seat cushion on his boat and wiped sweat from his brow.

"Come on over. Have a drink with me." Chad waved his arm in the air from his deck.

Nick wasn't in the mood, but thought hanging out with Chad might improve their noise wars. "Okay. Give me a few minutes to get organized."

Chad nodded and settled himself on a boat cushion with a drink in hand.

Nick picked up the books, carried them into his cabin and set them on the table. He'd have to study after having a drink with Chad. He put his helmet on the kitchen counter and rubbed the back of his neck, now a bit stiff from the motorcycle ride. Wishing he could rest, he went to the galley sink, splashed cold water on his face and wiped it with a towel. Making small conversation gave him knots in his stomach, the lingering fear of someone uncovering his fake identity. What in the world would they talk about? Reluctantly, he headed out to Chad's boat.

"Welcome aboard," Chad said as he rose from his chair. Nick shook his hand.

"What can I get you? How about a beer? Scotch? Vodka?"

"I'll take Scotch on the rocks." Nick managed a forced smile that pinched his face. Chad returned from the galley with a drink in each hand and offered one to Nick. "So, you got a job?"

"I did. Believe it or not, she was looking for a foreman." Nick took a swig.

"How's that?" Chad settled into a cushion and hoisted a leg up.

"Cassie said her foreman left on an emergency and was not coming back."

"Very convenient having you show up. Well, let's toast to your new job."

They clicked glasses. Nick tried to relax but he felt uneasy worrying Chad might ask him a lot of prying questions about his background.

"So, where ya' from?" Chad finished his drink, stood and poured another.

"Sort of everywhere. Sailing the islands."

Nick said, "How about you. Do I detect an Irish brogue?"

"Ah, the Irish is in me veins—from Northern Ireland. Small town, long ago."

Nick shifted in his seat, nerves now on edge. "How did you end up in Mallorca?"

"Always wanted to see these Balearic Islands—the weather's great most of the year. And you?"

"Same. I guess." Nick became agitated. His worst fear—small talk eventually led to too many questions about his past. He bit his upper lip and tried to relax.

Chad tried to coax Nick into a conversation. "Ever get married?"

"No. Never found the right woman. Found a woman I wanted, but someone else snatched her from under me." He fondly thought of Danielle, who fell in love with that bastard cop, Evan, who not only figured out his connection to a robbery at a bank in El Dorado Hills, California, but that he had also embezzled from the company and murdered its controller, Armond, to keep him for talking about it. He shook his head thinking of his thwarted plan to marry her and inherit Gaspard Yachting someday after Gaspard died. Unfortunately, his killing the whistle-blowing company controller put an end to that plan.

"And you?" Nick shifted to avoid the glare of the sun setting on the horizon.

Chad looked out with a wistful gaze over the sea. "Had me quite a woman. She died some years ago. Decided then to sail around."

"How long have you been here?" Nick finished his drink.

"About a year. I lose track of time, ya' know. What the hell day is it?"

Nick laughed. "I get that. Monday, Wednesday, all the same day."

"Let me get you another drink, okay?"

Nick accepted the offer. He scratched the back of his head, pushed off his sandals and put his feet up on the lounge cushion.

Chad returned with a drink for himself and one for Nick.

"That's one heck of a scar you've got there."

"War wound." Nick swallowed, then heaved a perturbed sigh.

Chad probed, "You in service?"

"Iraq. Army." Nick nervously rubbed the back of his neck.

18

"Shitty war, I heard."

Nick nodded, turned his leg and pointed to his calf. "Shrapnel souvenir."

When the conversation went dead, they sat in silence watching the sea and other boats rocking in the waves.

"So, tell me about this woman, at the hotel, what's her name again, Candy?"

"No, Cassie. She's very pretty, smart. An architect. She wants me to supervise the workers and keep the books."

"She the one who designed the hotel?" Chad stroked his chin.

"I don't know. Her father is an architect as well."

Chad asked, "Does he live here?"

"No, he's in Barcelona. Runs Benoit Construction."

Chad paused and snickered. "So, ya' working for a woman boss." The red veins in his bulbous noise seemed more prominent.

"Guess so. Beauty and brains."

He wiped his mustache. "I was surprised the building commission let them build another damn hotel on this island. Water is scarce."

"She told me they secured the building permit a couple of years ago. This is the last hotel they are allowing on the island."

"Good thing. We've got too many hotels here already—like nine million people coming here as tourists. It's gotten bloody crowded."

Nick nodded in agreement. They sat in silence sipping their drinks. Stars started appearing. Tourists and boat owners walked along the pier waving at them. People he didn't know and didn't want to know. "I think I've gotta' run. Got work to do before tomorrow."

Chad stood. "Glad you stopped by. Nice to spend time with ya'."

"Thanks for the invite." Nick set his glass on the table. "By the way, that's some baseball bat you have sitting in the corner. You play?"

19

"Naw. Here. Hold it." Chad handed the bat to Nick whose raised his eyebrows in surprise.

"Darn heavy. Like a Babe Ruth or Louisville Slugger," Nick said, handing the bat back to him.

"Keep it handy in case someone prowls around at night so I could beat the shit out of them. By the way, my TV bother you last night?" Chad stared at Nick.

Nick smiled. "Not so much. Thanks for keeping it down. Bothers me when the wind carries the noise. It was a pretty calm night."

Feeling mentally exhausted, Nick waved goodbye. For now, he dodged a bullet—no discussion about what he did before he came to Mallorca. Thank God. He boarded his boat, relieved to be home. Turned on the galley lights. How much reading could he manage before nodding off to sleep?

He decided to try to memorize the glossary of building terms to ensure he sounded knowledgeable about construction. A mild headache knotted in his forehead from the stress of chatting, but not one debilitating enough to require his migraine medication. Somehow, Chad had not asked him why he hadn't been out sailing recently. He didn't want to get into his cracked boom and engine trouble. Getting it fixed wasn't merely about the expense. If they had to drydock the boat, he'd have to live in a hotel and move his belongings. Stuff he didn't want to worry about with a new job on the horizon.

CHAPTER 5
Evan and Danielle

Evan drove their rental car to the hotel concerned about the engine light flickering—something he'd have to take care of after they got settled. He drove up to the portico. A bellman opened Danielle's side of the door and offered his hand to help her out of the car. "Welcome to the *Calatrava*," he said, his face sporting a broad smile.

Evan set their luggage on the curb and walked into the hotel with Danielle. She glanced up at the towering ceiling of rustic beams and wrought-iron chandeliers, then scanned the travertine floor and comfy-looking caramel and sapphire fabric club chairs. The receptionist at the desk told them their room number and gave Evan a key and a second one for Danielle.

They walked to the elevator and were pleased they were on the fifteenth floor. The halls were carpeted in a deep indigo and beige harlequin design. Fresh orchids in decorative pots sat on massive stone consoles, and beautiful brass and glass sconces cast a warm glow on deep beige walls. Their room was down a long hallway past the ice machine. Evan put his card in the door and told her to close her eyes. He guided her into the middle of the room.

"Okay, open your eyes." She momentarily stood there, glancing around the room, the vaulted ceilings and their luxurious surroundings. The massive king-size bed and fluffy duvet beckoned. Across the room sat a huge chest of drawers and a writing desk. Facing the glass doors was a sitting room with a sofa, two chairs and a glass coffee table. Enchanted, she twirled and ran to the open terrace.

"Oh, my Lord. It's beautiful! The view of the sea from here is spectacular. This huge terrace with a bistro table and chairs is perfect for breakfast or a late-night glass of wine. I just love it!" She put her arms around Evan and gave him a lingering kiss. He kissed her back with intensity to give her something to think about until they went to bed.

"I'm glad you like it. I thought it would be wonderful to sleep in front of a terrace with the breezes blowing at night."

"I agree." She plopped down on the bed. "Very comfortable."

He offered her his hand. "You hungry?"

"Starved. Let's go to a nice restaurant in town. I'd love to see Mallorca at night and I'm anxious to try some of their local food."

"Great! I read the travel brochure on the plane. How about the Caimari? It's a renovated country house with authentic home cooking and a six-course meal. Will that fill you up?"

She laughed. "You know how I love to eat. What do you want to do tomorrow?"

"I thought we could take a coast drive up the Tramuntana, then head back and have lunch at some trendy outdoor café in Palma."

The bellman rang their door bell and brought in the luggage. Evan tipped him handsomely. He thanked Evan and quietly left.

Evan asked, "You want to change for dinner?"

"Yes. Let me take a shower and freshen up. Why don't you take a nap? I'll wake you when I'm ready." Danielle offered.

"I could join you in the shower." He winked at her.

"Now there's a good idea." Danielle began undressing.

CHAPTER 6
Nick

Nick stayed up until 1:00 a.m. studying in the kitchen galley. He had memorized construction terms, learned a great deal about how hotels were built, and felt he could manage the new software for tracking expenditures and deliveries from Spain. Cassie had mentioned that many items were manufactured on the island, but the specialty hardware fixtures and furnishings were coming from Spain.

He stacked his books on a corner bench and turned off the galley lights. He took a quick shower and dried off with a large towel that would still be damp in the morning. Realizing he had not eaten, he headed barefoot into the kitchen with the towel tucked around his hips. He liked his corner galley with a stove, microwave and large prep area. Inspecting the contents of the refrigerator, he was unsure of what he had stashed in there the day before. He found some leftover pasta in tomato cream sauce from a favorite restaurant. That and a glass of merlot would do.

After dinner he donned a pair of briefs and crawled into bed. Lights from other boats shown through his portholes. He pitched open a window next to the bed. Fresh, salty air breezed in. As he lay there, he thought about the day.

What were the chances he'd land a job on the first try? However, he did a lot of accounting work and marketing for Gaspard—it wasn't like he didn't have skills, not to mention building expensive yachts. That wasn't what worried him.

He figured he could learn on the job from the workers who had been entrenched in the project for months. However, one thing bothered him. What if Cassie looked him up on the Internet? He never thought to ask his drug-running buddies to create a fake Internet identity. Shit. He rose, started up his laptop and sent an email to Cruz asking him to create a fake website for himself and a pseudo one for his father's construction company with dates indicating the closure about two years ago. He knew searching the Internet to find someone was useless unless one had a web page or was noteworthy, posting or blogging—otherwise one didn't show up, of course unless one was a criminal.

He Googled *Nick Fontaine.* Several names showed up. A musician at the New York Symphony, a lawyer, and a body builder. If pressed, he could claim to be doing body builder work because he did have a strong physique. He could feel his temples pulsing with worry, and didn't want anything to go wrong. He cringed when he thought of his young life—with his abusive, alcoholic father and his brilliant but deranged brother, Ted, who orchestrated a bank robbery-gone-wrong in El Dorado Hill, California four years ago. He tried to put that horrible shooting behind him. Ted accidentally shot Evan's little sister, who later died, and Evan, the off-duty cop who happened to be there, shot Ted in the leg. They didn't get the bullet out in time, it got infected and then septic. Ted died a few weeks after the robbery.

Poor kids–they both had a lousy life. Whenever he thought of Ted, he recalled horrific memories of them as two starving kids, stuck in a pitch-dark underground cellar with no food for days except for a skinned roasted squirrel tossed in by their father. He was surprised he didn't turn out to be a serial killer. Yes, he made disastrous mistakes. He'd lost his temper and killed the controller who threatened to blow his cover to Gaspard, his partner and the owner of the yachting company. That mistake continued to haunt him.

Living on Mallorca was starting over. He didn't want a life as a criminal on the run and didn't think of himself as a bad guy—just a misfortunate and crafty one who avoided being caught. As he dozed in bed, he began to hear the dreaded noise of Chad's TV. He shook his head in disgust. Of all nights to have so much racket. He needed sleep before going to work. He thought of the bat. With that bat he could smash the damn TV. He grabbed the loose pillow next to him and put it over his head to drown out the noise and hoped he'd get at least six hours sleep.

CHAPTER 7
Evan and Danielle

On the drive up the winding Tramuntana road, Evan and Danielle laughed about being too exhausted to go out to dinner after their risqué coupling in the shower. They'd ordered room service instead, had a nightcap of a local Cabernet, and sat on the terrace enjoying the soft breeze.

"Gosh, it's beautiful! These cliffs overlooking the sea are stunning," Danielle said. "The water is such a deep azure blue and there's not a cloud in the sky."

"There's a restaurant I wanted to try along the way. Mirador de Ricardo Roca comes highly recommended. You hungry?" Evan asked.

"Absolutely." Danielle twisted her auburn hair around her finger to keep it from flying out the open car window.

They drove the switchback turns with ease and Evan said, "I'm glad you don't get carsick. By the way, I read you can rent mopeds to tour the island. Are you game?"

"Sure. That would be fun! I'll remember not to wear a sundress."

As they climbed, the air became markedly cooler. Danielle shivered. "I should have brought a wrap."

Evan rubbed her shoulder. "I'll make sure we get a table in the sun to keep you warm."

Danielle smiled and glanced at Evan. "I feel so much better after our Facetime conversation with Mama. Trevor looked so cute in his pajamas, smiling and giggling. Kelly is such a dear woman to have flown in from California just to be with Marie. Both of our mothers get along so well. We are so blessed. I feel much more relaxed knowing Trevor isn't afraid."

"He'll be just fine. No worries." Evan added.

They stopped at Valldemossa, where Frederic Chopin wintered, strolled through the town's narrow alleys, visited the monastery and royal palace. Lunch at Mirador de Ricardo Roca proved to be an excellent suggestion. Evan feasted on fresh lobster and Danielle tried a local dish of tumbet de peix, a pie made of white fish, peppers, eggplant and eggs.

Evan poured more butter on his lobster. "Remember when we first met?"

"How could I forget? I literally fell at your feet, my students' papers flying every which way. You helped me pick up the scattered mess, and then you convinced me to stop and have a coffee and pastry with you."

"You were the most beautiful creature I'd ever seen. I was smitten the moment I saw you." He reached over and placed his hand on hers.

Evan paid the bill, left a nice tip and used his high school Spanish to say *Gracias* and *Adios*. Being the ever-considerate gentlemen, he pulled Danielle's chair away from the table and helped her up. They walked arm in arm down the cascade of stone steps from the restaurant to their rental car.

Danielle stared at Evan while he drove, the cleft in his chin and his dark hair blowing in the breeze made him so handsome.

"I knew it was destiny when we met. I'm so happy being married to you, Evan. I couldn't imagine a better life. I love you so much."

"I love you more," Evan said, while he rounded another hairpin turn climbing higher, driving through tunnels of ancient stone, the temperature cooling even further. When they were nearing the end of the drive, Danielle noticed the construction and a sign, *Cielo*. Ever curious she said, "Let's stop and see what's being built."

"Sure." Evan parked the car on the side of the gravel road. It seemed they had reached a pinnacle where the main road stopped. He opened the door for her and helped her out of the car. They walked to the edge of the road and admired the view from the promontory. Large sailboats and yachts became tiny white dots on the sea. A cruise ship was headed toward Palma. They turned and walked up the gravel path to the construction site.

"Oh, it's going to be a hotel," Danielle said. She noticed a bevy of construction workers milling about, insulation and drywall being installed with nail guns hammering. Wishing she had worn something other than sandals, she maneuvered past tall trees stepping carefully around small boulders and loose stones. Her heart nearly stopped when she spotted a man with bleached blond hair talking to a group of workers. Evan was looking in a different direction. Chills ran down her spine. Her knees felt like they would buckle. He looked like Ryan Coltrane with very blond hair and a scruffy beard. No, it couldn't be! Perhaps she was wrong. The man turned and walked away. Suddenly light-headed with fear, she grabbed Evan's arm.

"I'm really cold. Could we please go back to the car?"

Evan glanced at her. "Are you okay? You're as pale as a ghost."

"I feel lightheaded—like I might faint," she said barely audible.

"Might be the altitude and hiking up here after eating. Let's get you back to the car. I wish I had a jacket to offer you."

He rolled up the windows to keep the draft from coming inside the car.

She held her stomach, fearful the contents might erupt. Although always honest with Evan, she knew there was no way she could tell him who she thought she saw.

CHAPTER 8
Danielle

Danielle was unusually quiet on the way back to the hotel. She was still shivering from the shock of seeing someone who might be Ryan. How could it be him?

Supposedly dead from the blast of blowing up his yacht in Nice, but now alive?

She never kept secrets from Evan, except when she was pregnant, and learned the hard way how it angered him almost to the point of their breaking up. She bit her lip and wrapped her hands around her arms to stop them from shaking. Hopefully, Evan would assume she was coming down with something. If she told Evan who she thought she saw, he would ditch his artist life, become a cop again and pursue Ryan 'till the end of the earth.

He often told her, after the explosion, that he didn't believe Ryan was dead. What if Ryan was still alive? What would happen? Danielle feared Evan would confront Ryan and want to extradite him back to Nice, or worse, El Dorado Hills, California where Evan had been a detective and the robbery occurred where his six-year old sister and others had been killed in the shootout during the robbers' escape. How do you bring a dead man back to life? Evan would have to involve the local police. She knew if Ryan saw Evan on this island, Ryan would flee, or he'd try to kill Evan because there was no way Ryan was going to prison. She pondered the situation and wondered what was Ryan doing at the hotel construction site? He seemed to be working there. It made no sense.

She snuggled into the seat while Evan turned on the heat to warm her up. Thirty minutes or so in good traffic and they would be back at the hotel. Her heart ached—she wanted to tell Evan the truth about who she saw, or who she thought she saw, but also wanted to protect the man she loved.

She thought back to those days before Ryan blew up his yacht. As part of his escape plan, he'd captured Lena, her younger sister, and taken her hostage on a raft, wrapped her with duct-tape and a flashlight and left her in the middle of the ocean. Her father, Gaspard, had received a text message, along with the Nice police specifying where to pick her up. Ryan had drugged Lena using her as bait so Evan and the Coast Guard could see the explosion of his yacht and think he was dead. Although she didn't die, she had been drugged and suffered from a post-traumatic stress condition that took her a long time to recover. For someone who loved swimming in the ocean, Lena became paralyzed with fear if she closed her eyes while in the water. Evan had saved her from drowning—Evan and his former boss, Sheriff Cosley, and the Coast Guard all helped to save Lena. Although Ryan apparently had no intent to kill Lena, she could have been seriously injured if she had remained in the raft when Ryan blew up his yacht. Danielle winced at her memory of this event.

Evan interrupted her thoughts. "You okay? You're so quiet." He looked at her with concern.

"I'm fine now. We're almost at our hotel."

"How about if we go up to our room, change clothes and relax at the beach?"

"Sounds good."

"You sure you're okay?"

"I'm fine." She forced a contrived happy smile and took his arm, unsure about how long she could keep this secret from him.

CHAPTER 9
Nick

"No, dammit, no!" Nick said as he rubbed the side of his temple. Blood throbbed in his veins and he felt his hair stand up on the back of his neck. Was that really Danielle he saw standing up on the hill? The first day of work had been going so well. He'd met the crew, mostly island workers who were pleasant to him, welcoming, in fact. His boss, Cassandra, gave him a work t-shirt, with a logo of the new hotel, *Cielo*, and she showed him how to manage the spreadsheets and accounting records. Now busy in her own office space in the trailer, he went to a separate space at the opposite end of the interior to do his work. What were the odds that Danielle would be on this island? Shit. If she was here, then the man with his back to me had to be Evan. What in the hell were they doing on this island? Worse yet, how long would they be here?

Nick walked outside the trailer and was interrupted by one of the workers who told him the trusses were being lifted into place to frame the ceiling of the hotel. He thanked the worker, then went back to a state of agitation he had not experienced since he left Gaspard Yachting and fled to Mallorca. He could feel a migraine starting, the aura and throbbing beginning a slow, relentless pounding in the front of his forehead. He inhaled a deep breath, trying to remain calm. Thoughts ran through his head like a speeding train. Had Danielle and Evan shown up any other time—a time when he didn't have a damn job he just started, he could hide out on his sailboat until they were gone, or even sail to another island. But, no! Now he had dead minnows stinking up his boat and clogging his engine, a cracked boom; a sailboat not seaworthy until these two things were fixed.

He went back inside the trailer to the restroom, and used a cold paper towel to dab his forehead. Fortunately, Cassie was not in the trailer. She'd gone into town to review the construction of the permanent sign for the hotel. Her being gone was a blessing. However, shaving most of his beard off, a disaster in timing, he now looked like his old self as Ryan Coltrane instead of Nick Fontaine. He shook his head in disbelief. This couldn't be happening. Just when he thought he was done being pursued by Evan, it could start all over again. No way was he going to prison. He went to the trailer refrigerator and grabbed a Coke. The sugar and caffeine would help his migraine until he could get home to his sailboat where he kept his medication. He sat at his desk breathing deeply and chewing his upper lip. His hands were clammy from stress, like an adrenaline rush where you had a fight-or flight syndrome. He'd have to logically think this through.

If Evan and Danielle were on the island, it could mean Gaspard brought them on the *Belle Chloe*, his treasured, favorite yacht. Could anything be worse? Or, it could mean the entire family was here with Gaspard. How long would they be here? Days? A week? More? He gulped down the Coke. Or, maybe only Danielle and Evan were here on vacation. That would require some sneaky investigation, and with all the hotels on this island, they could be staying anywhere. If Gaspard didn't bring his yacht here, then they wouldn't be in the marina. If they weren't in the marina, then Evan and Danielle wouldn't be running into him.

All this to worry about made Nick bristle with fear—the kind of fear that brought on shingles on top of migraines. Beyond frustrating. He'd just started a new job, he couldn't bolt and leave Cassie in the lurch. He had to show up for work. If he didn't come to work, he'd have to hang around on his boat, the one place Evan and Danielle didn't know where he lived.

He finished entering the records for the shipments of drywall that arrived, and shrugged off the fatal fear mode he was in. Since it was nearly 4:00, he'd be heading home soon. Stopping at a restaurant on the way home to grab some takeout food was something he usually did, but now he couldn't take the risk. He was worried that Evan and Danielle might be at a restaurant. If he made it home without being spotted, he'd don dark sunglasses and a Panama hat when he went out.

Cassie's voice outside the trailer alerted him that she was back. She seemed to be busy with the sheetrock installer, so he left the trailer, waved to her and said "See 'ya tomorrow." She nodded and continued her conversation.

He walked to his motorcycle, and put on his helmet thinking at least no one in the Gaspard DuBois family would recognize him if he was seen riding, including Danielle or Evan.

He raced down the hairpin turns leaning into the curves, weaving around traffic on the two-lane road. Now anger set in; boiling, frustrating anger. Time to take out his Glock and put a clip in when he got back to his boat.

CHAPTER 10
Cassie

After a long day's work, Cassie grabbed a ham sandwich from her tote and sat down at her desk. On the wall behind her desk was a huge design board filled with carpeting, fabric and leather swatches for the lobby and individual guest rooms, photos of chandeliers, and several paint samples for room colors. She moved a pile of invoices to the corner of her desk, put her feet up on a desk drawer and tried to relax. Tomorrow she'd give the stack of unpaid bills to Nick to enter into the spreadsheets. For now, she wished she had a glass of Pinot Noir to go with her sandwich, but she wasn't going to drive the hairpin turns of the Tramantuna back to her hotel after drinking wine.

Her cell phone pinged. "Hi, Dad, how are you?"

"I'm good. How's the progress?"

"Everything is going well. I met with the sign manufacturing company for the front of the hotel. The design is really great. Oh, and I hired a replacement for Fernando."

"He was your foreman, right?"

"Yes. His wife is very ill. They have two small kids. He's going to stay at home with her."

"Sorry to hear it. I hope everything will be okay. You're still at the office?"

"I was sorting through the invoices for tomorrow's data entry. For now we're on budget, but there are huge expenses coming up."

"How did you find a new foreman so quickly?"

"That was serendipity. This guy, Nick, shows up looking for a job the day I lost Fernando."

"Has he worked in the hotel industry before?"

"No, but he seemed like a nice enough guy, worked for his father's construction company building houses and keeping the books."

"Do you want me to check him out?"

"Yeah, that would be a good idea. It's not like he had a resumé with him, and I didn't ask for one. I panicked when Fernando resigned and didn't want to get behind on the construction."

"What's the guy's name?"

"Nick Fontaine—lives on his boat in the marina."

"Okay. I'll check him out. What was the name of the company his dad owned?"

"No idea. I didn't ask. He's a contract employee like most of the other workers, so if he doesn't work out, it's not a problem, I'll just let him go."

"How do you like working in the trailer?"

"It's great. Been used for other hotel construction jobs. Thanks for getting it for me—I have an office and Nick is at the other end of the trailer so we don't bother each other."

"Good to hear. I'll call you when I have something. Don't work too late."

"I won't, Dad."

Cassie sat back in her chair with a bit of self-recrimination for hiring someone without doing a background check. But Nick's timing was so fortuitous she took it as a good omen and an answer to an unspoken prayer. Plus, he was engaging, charming and very attractive. How could she say no? She prided herself on her intuition and didn't like making mistakes. She was absolutely sure Nick was a good hire.

CHAPTER 11
Evan and Danielle

Trade wind breezes blew into their room creating a balmy atmosphere. With the terrace doors wide open, a full moon cast long shadows on the carpet. Despite the comfort of their bed and the fluffy duvet, Danielle could not sleep. Seeing someone who looked like Ryan set off tremors of terror. She was grateful Evan assumed she was under the weather and did not press for a romantic interlude. He had kissed her with his usual fervor, but understood she probably wasn't feeling well after the hike up to *Cielo*. Now in a deep sleep, his arm was curled across her waist, his lips brushing against her neck made her even more upset. This man was everything she ever wanted in a husband except for his past relentless pursuit of a criminal he thought was still alive. For her sake, Evan had set aside his badge and promised to assume Ryan was dead. As newlyweds, their life now focused on his successful career as an artist, his teaching art to children at her school, and their young child, Trevor. How could she tell him he might be right—that Ryan was still alive.

She lifted Evan's arm from her waist, turned and kissed him lightly on the forehead. This was the most difficult dilemma she had ever faced. Of course, she could be wrong. Maybe the man she saw only looked like Ryan, but was someone else. Because she didn't know for sure, she crafted a plan.

After their swim in the ocean, Evan had told her earlier in the evening that he felt something was wrong with their rental car—the flashing red light indicated an oil issue that needed to be resolved, so he wanted to exchange the car in the morning for another one, and planned to drive to the airport car rental. He asked her if she wanted to come along, but she had told him she wanted to relax by the pool. Instead, she was planning on calling information to see if there was a phone number for *Cielo*. Surely if she contacted the person in charge, she could find out if Ryan Coltrane was working there. At least she would know for sure, and then could decide what to tell Evan. Danielle closed her weary eyes and drifted off to a fitful sleep.

They both woke around 8:00. He nestled his head at the back of her neck, his hand stroking her thigh. She could tell he wanted to make love to her, and she didn't want to go through the motions of lovemaking while unable to concentrate on pleasing him or herself. His dark curly hair toppled over his forehead and she brushed it aside and kissed him lightly. "Morning sleepy head," he said while stroking the small of her back. She responded with a sigh and curled into him. "You still plan on taking in the rental car this morning?"

"I need to get another car. The one we have now has an oil problem. It could stall on one of the remote roads. You sure you don't want to come along?"

"No, it's fine. I have a good book to read and want to lounge around the pool."

"You feeling okay?" Evan's concern was evident in his voice.

"I'm fine. Much better today. Hungry actually."

"Of course, you are. You never had dinner last night."

"You're right. Let's order room service breakfast and sit on the terrace."

Evan slid his legs to the side of the bed and sat up. "Sounds good." She knew he had no idea what she planned to do once he was gone.

CHAPTER 12
Danielle and Cassandra

No sooner was Evan out the door on the way to the car rental when Danielle found her phone and dialed information. "Do you have a phone number for the *Cielo* hotel? It's under construction and I need to reach someone there."

The operator had her wait a few minutes and then gave her the number. She took a deep breath and dialed.

A woman answered the phone. "This is Cassandra Benoit. Can I help you?"

"Uh, my name is Danielle Wentworth. I need to ask you about one of your workers, Ryan Coltrane. I think I saw him on your property yesterday."

"I'm sorry, but there is no one working here by that name."

"Are you sure? Danielle pressed. "He's the one with the bleached blond hair."

"Oh, you must be mistaken. That's Nick Fontaine. What's this about?"

"It's complicated, but you could be in danger."

Cassandra's voice sounded perplexed. "Why would you say that?"

"He probably changed his name. Ryan used to work for my father at Gaspard Yachting, in Nice, was his partner, in fact, and murdered our controller. He blew up his yacht and faked his death."

"Seriously? I think you have the wrong person."

"Maybe, but my husband is a retired cop, and if he finds out Ryan is still alive, he will want to arrest him or come after him in some way. I think I saw Ryan yesterday when we were touring the area. I mean, it might not be him, but he looks just like him."

"Well, people have look-alike doubles and I'm sure you're wrong."

"Could I please speak to him?" Danielle pleaded, her voice now shaking.

"No, he's on the far side of the construction. Can I have him call you?"

"Uh, um, no. That's okay. Do you have his phone number?"

"Yes, but I don't want to give it out to a stranger."

"I'm sure you think I'm nuts, but if he really is Ryan Coltrane, would you want him working for you? You need to be careful. He's a bank robber and murderer and he's embezzled money." Danielle's voice cracked under the stress.

"I have to go now," Cassandra said. "A delivery truck is here."

Casandra hung up. Danielle sat there, shaking, tears welling up in her eyes. What was she thinking? She was sure she sounded like a crazy person. Of course, she couldn't have left him a message. She didn't want Ryan to know she saw him. It never occurred to her that he saw her as well. If so, was Evan in danger? Probably not. This Ryan/Nick person didn't know where they were staying, and, she certainly couldn't risk having Cassandra returning her call when Evan was around.

Danielle knew Evan was going to be very upset with her for making this call.

CHAPTER 13
Cassandra and Nick

Cassandra sat back in her office chair, baffled by the preposterous call. Who was this woman? Danielle, something, trying to get her to believe a harrowing story about one of her new hires. Nick was doing a very good job so far, arriving to work on time, keeping track of the workers, receiving shipments and entering in the financial information on their computer ledgers. She decided this woman had to be a lunatic, but nevertheless, she dialed her father at the office.

"Hey, dad."

"Cassie. Good to hear from you. Everything okay?"

"Yeah, but I wonder if you had a chance to check out Nick Fontaine?"

"I did. I was going to call you later today, but you got to me first."

"Well?" Cassie bit the inside of her cheek.

"Seems fine. I found *Nick Fontaine*, a body builder, and another with that name, a symphony player, and at last, a lawyer, but eventually I found a website for Fontaine construction. Mentions Justin Fontaine, deceased. Appears the company was sold by his son, Nick, about two years ago. That helpful?"

"More than you know. Some crazy woman called me today with a far-fetched story about Nick being someone else. Can't be too careful, but Nick is doing a really good job."

"What's the status with the hotel?" Roberto asked.

"Coming along. The trusses are in, tile roof is nearly installed, electrical work is done and walls are insulated. Sheet rocking should be done this week. What about the furniture?"

"Beds, desks and mini-bars all ordered. I won't release these until you are ready. Furniture has a 10-week lead time. Have you selected the color scheme?"

"I'm thinking pale dusty aqua for the walls, to soothe the senses and invite the seaside in, lots of off-white and amber accents. I have the sinks and faucets identified, the marble flooring and the ceiling fans picked out. I still have to select club chairs and sofas for the sitting rooms. How about deep teal for the chairs, rust, teal and an amber print for the sofas and window coverings. I haven't decided on the carpeting or the granite for the reception desk."

"Sounds lovely, honey."

"Everything set for the waterfall and spa massage tables?"

"Yes, and for the bedding, towels, and ice machines. I got a great discount."

"Oh, I meant to tell you," she added. "The construction for the outdoor swimming pool is nearly done. Rebar is completed. They should finish it this month."

"Okay. Stay in touch. Let me know if you need anything."

"Will do. Love you dad."

"You, too, honey."

Cassandra sat by her desk and breathed a sigh of relief. This crazy woman gave her a lot to be concerned about—calling with such a hairbrained story. Whoever she thought Nick was, he wasn't. She glanced out her trailer window and noticed the sky had turned ominous. Dark clouds were moving in quickly, a storm brewing out on the horizon. At this time of year, storms were mild. The hotel was nearly finished. If they had to, workers would tarp over the unfinished roofing.

She poured another cup of coffee from the coffee maker, added two packets of sugar, and two creams. She disliked the taste of coffee, but loved the caffeine buzz it gave her. Lightning crackled in the distance, the storm moving closer. Everything was coming together for the hotel on schedule—a storm wouldn't ruin anything. She glanced outside and watched workers cover up lumber and marble with tarps, most of which had already been brought indoors. Relaxing with her coffee, she thought about whether or not to talk to Nick about the bizarre phone call. At first, she decided not to bother him, and then, on second thought she felt he should know someone stopped by here yesterday, thought he was someone else, and made these unfounded claims about who he really was. She shook her head in disbelief and decided to wait for him. Thunder rattled her nerves. Being on a promontory, and closer to the sky, weather always seemed more severe. Rain now began to pelt the trailer making it sound like a giant tin can. She turned to look at her carpeting swatches and heard the trailer door open.

"God, it's raining hard out there," Nick said shaking off his arms, dripping water on the trailer floor. "I sent the crew home for the day, as there's not much to be done outside anyway. Those working inside will finish in an hour."

Cassandra ruffled through a pile of paperwork. "I have a stack of invoices for you. Enter them when you can. I've paid all of them, made adjustments where there were errors."

He walked over to her desk, took the invoices and sat down in a chair.

"I wanted to tell you I'm pleased with the crew—very conscientious, not wasting any time, steady workers."

She smiled at him. "Glad to hear it."

"What's up? You look like you have something to say?"

"I had a really frightening call today from a woman, Danielle something. Said she saw you here yesterday and claimed you are someone else—Ryan Coltrane."

Nick hid his fear, but his heart nearly stopped. "Oh, really?"

"She claimed you worked for her father, embezzled money, and said something about blowing up your yacht to fake your identity."

"That all?" Nick laughed.

"I mean, can you believe it?" She must know someone who looks a lot like you.

Nick shivered. "Well, I'm sorry she upset you. Geez. Do you think I look like a killer?"

"Of course not. I did have you checked out on the Internet. My dad did it for me. Everything seemed fine. Said your dad, Justin, died and you sold the company a couple of years ago. So, you're the legacy of Fontaine Construction?"

"Guess so. Did you want me to enter those invoices before I leave?"

"That would be great," she said and stood up from her chair walking behind him. He stood as well, close enough to her to pick up a scent of her perfume.

A bit of awkward maneuvering around one another, his hand lightly brushed hers as she walked by. They stood looking at one another, and then she laughed and said, "I'll see you tomorrow."

Nick took the invoices to his desk, sat down and felt the blood drain from his veins. His head was pounding. A terrible migraine would ensue if he didn't take his preventive medication which he didn't have with him. He rubbed his temples and the back of his head, massaging the skin to try to break up the pain cycle. His worst fear came to pass. That idiot woman, Danielle, had the gall to call Cassandra. Obviously, Cruz, his buddy, had put up a fake identity for him on the Internet, and one for his father, using another fake name, Justin Fontaine. He'd now have to remember his fake father's name, along with being Nick Fontaine instead of Ryan Coltrane, the name he used at Gaspard's Yachting. None of these names were even close to his real birth name, Jed Reddiger. Getting too damn hard to remember who he was supposed to be—too easy for slipups.

What was he to do now about Danielle and Evan? He had several choices, none of which were good. If he bolted from his job this afternoon, he couldn't take his boat and sail to another island; it still needed repair. Not to mention, there was a nasty storm, lousy for sailing and his sailboat was inoperable with a cracked boom and engine clogged with minnows. Besides, if his boat were operable, where would he sail to? Assuming his boat was seaworthy and there wasn't a storm, he could sail to Menorca or Ibiza, both possible places he could hide out until Evan and Danielle left the island. How long could that be? A couple of weeks? A month? The odds were Evan and Danielle were on vacation and would not be here very long.

Another option would be to quit his job with Cassie, and simply hide out on his boat at the marina. Evan would have no idea he lived on a boat, and certainly might have assumed he bought a yacht and not a sailboat. Evan wouldn't be looking for 49' Hunter moored in the marina. He'd have to think this through, but unless he entered the invoices now, his head would cause such intractable pain, he'd never be able to concentrate.

An hour later after downing three Coca Colas, and grateful for the caffeine buzz and widening of his arteries, he finished the invoices. Rain pounded, slanting sideways in windy torrents. He turned off the lights, locked up the trailer and headed for his motorcycle. No doubt he'd be soaking wet, but in a good way, the wind and rain would cool him off. After today's explosion of pain, he decided he'd have to keep his migraine medication with him, assuming he'd be returning to work. Of course, if he didn't show up, Cassie would be alarmed and might decide Danielle was telling the truth.

He drove cautiously, his motorcycle wheels spinning sideways on the turns, a careful boot nearing the road when necessary for balance.

He wiped his helmet and could see the marina, boats slamming into piers, other boats rocking wildly in the storm. He parked his cycle, ran to his boat and ensured it was tightly moored to the pier cleats. His clothing was drenched. He shivered, unlocked his galley door and sat down on the cushions. Two migraine medications were downed with a half glass of brandy. He tossed his clothing in a heap, dried off with two towels and laid down in bed. Not the worst day of his life, but close. He reached in his nightstand and fingered his Glock, the clip now in place. Not likely he was going to get much sleep fuming over today's events.

CHAPTER 14
Evan and Danielle

Danielle heard the room key in the door and took a deep breath, frightened and anxious about what she had done, perhaps making a call she shouldn't have made.

"Hey, sweetie. You're starting to get a really nice tan. I'm glad you don't look as ghostly white as you did yesterday," Evan said.

"Did you get us a different car?"

"Yes. The car rental company was very accommodating and gave me a replacement. It's a bright red Renault."

Danielle forced a smile. "Hon, I think you need to sit down. I have something to tell you."

Evan grabbed a cold beer from the hotel mini-bar and sat on the sofa.

"You're not pregnant, are you?" he said with a teasing wink.

"No, I wish it were that simple." Danielle frowned and sat down on the sofa next to Evan.

"Remember when I wasn't feeling well yesterday? Well, I, um, panicked. I thought I saw Ryan. He was standing with a group of workers at the construction site."

"Are you sure? Why didn't you say something?" Evan gritted his teeth.

"It was such a shock. He had really blond hair, but I thought it was Ryan.

"Shit. I should go back up there right away." Evan bolted up from the sofa and began pacing around the sitting room. "See, I told you when he blew up his yacht he wasn't dead."

Danielle stood and faced Evan. "It could be someone else who looks like Ryan, but that's not all I wanted to tell you. I did something I shouldn't have done without asking you first."

Evan turned to her, his face a contorted frown. "So, what did you do?"

"I, um, called the *Cielo* hotel and talked to a woman, Cassandra, I think, and I asked her if she had someone named Ryan Coltrane working there.

Evan put his hand on her shoulder, "You did what?"

"I know, I shouldn't have called." Danielle bit the top of her lip.

"Well, what did she say?" Evan shook his head in frustration.

"She said she didn't have anyone by that name working there—the person I saw was Nick Fontaine."

Evan, furious, tried to control his anger. "I'm really upset with you.

If you had told me before you called, I could have strategized on how to handle this. What you've done now is blown any chance of confronting him if he is Ryan.

Did you ever think if he saw you, he probably is already on the run?"

Danielle started trembling. "That's not the worst of what I have done."

Evan rubbed his chin and clenched his teeth. "There's more? What more could there be?"

"I told Cassandra what Ryan had done, that he was a cold-blooded killer, and an embezzler of my father's company, and that if this person was Ryan, she might be in danger."

Evan yelled, "Unbelievable! I can't believe you didn't think this through. This was my case, and mine to decide how to proceed. You should know better. You're not the cop in this family."

Danielle started to cry in hiccup sobs. "I'm so sorry—I, uh, wanted to protect you. I knew you'd do something rash. You promised me you'd let Ryan's death go—you didn't find a body after his yacht exploded, and yes, he probably faked his death, but we agreed to get on with our lives. This is our belated honeymoon. We waited over a year to be by ourselves, and now this."

Evan moved away from her and walked toward the terrace, his arms folded in frustration.

The air in the room seemed to engulf her in fear and she didn't know what to do to make this situation less upsetting. She'd never seen Evan this angry. Lighting crackled in the background followed by a loud thunder clap. Rain began to pour onto the terrace.

Danielle winced, putting the back of her hand to her forehead. "What are you going to do?"

"I don't know. I have half a mind to get in the car and drive up there to see for myself if it weren't for this impending storm." He walked out to the covered terrace and put his hands on the balcony railing. "Besides, this late in the afternoon, everyone working at *Cielo* has probably gone home."

She followed him and put her hand on his shoulder. "Evan, please don't. If he sees you, he will flee, or worse yet, he might try to kill you."

"You should've thought of that before making that call. I'm really upset with you, Danielle. After all we've been through, you know what it would mean for me to set things right. Ashley, who was only six years old, died because of Ryan and that horrible bank robbery gone wrong—it's a justice I still owe her, a justice that alluded me when Ryan blew up his yacht. There's not a day that goes by that I don't think of her, still feel responsible—I should have protected her, but instead rogue bullets sprayed her side of the car—she never had a chance."

She turned toward him. "You don't have to do this, Evan. We have a wonderful life, and we have a child. You have to think of Trevor. If something happens to you—"

Evan turned toward her. "You should have thought of that before you made the call. If he *is* alive, I can't let this go."

"I was so frightened when I saw him, I didn't think."

Evan brushed past her in dismay, shaking his head.

"Where are you going?" Danielle asked.

"I don't know. I'm going to take a walk. Think this through." He left the room. The door slammed and then clicked into place.

Danielle bit her lip and tried to control her sobs. Perhaps if she had told Evan the moment she saw Ryan, things would have gone differently. He would have confronted Ryan, right then and there, or the person who might not be Ryan, and it could have ended. Chills ran down her spine. Maybe this person really was Nick Fontaine. She shivered, sat on the bed and put her head in her hands

Hours later, Danielle heard Evan return to their room. She was lying on the bed, pretending to be asleep. She could hear him undressing, keys rattling, shoes dropping to the floor. He sat on the edge of the bed and then laid down. She turned toward him. "I'm so sorry," she said, "really sorry."

"I know you are, but that doesn't change anything." He stretched out on the bed putting his arms behind his head. "I picked up a sandwich for you. It's on the dresser."

"Did you eat?"

"No. Not hungry." He turned over and shut off the light next to the bed.

For a long time, Danielle stared at the ceiling. They never had such a bad fight—and on their belated year-long wait for a honeymoon of all places. What she'd done was unforgivable. She wished she could have handled things differently but her emotions clouded her judgement. At some point, she drifted off to sleep, a troubled sleep that left her fretting about what she knew she would do. Knowing Evan was a deep sleeper now snoring loudly, she got up, quietly packed a few of her clothes. She took her phone into the bathroom, shut the door and made a phone call to the front desk to schedule a taxi for early in the morning. Another phone call to the airlines ensured she was able to change her return flight.

In the morning when Evan awoke, he found her letter:

"Evan, there is nothing I can say to make the situation better. I understand your need to bring justice for Ashley's death, but this is a very dangerous justice. If something happens to you, I will be raising Trevor by myself. I can't stay on this island and watch you get killed. Because you were a cop, and always will be, I would only be in the way. I would try to stop you from doing what you need to do. I'm going home while you sort this out. I love you more than life itself. If you can forgive me, you know where I'll be—waiting and hoping you can find your way back to me. All my love, always, Danielle."

CHAPTER 15
Evan

The storm passed leaving messy palm fronds on the hotel room's terrace. The air felt electrified and clean. A small lizard scooted across the tile. Evan held Danielle's letter in his hands and read it again. Although he was no longer as angry with her for making the phone call, he was dumbfounded and upset that she would leave him and fly home to St. Paul-de-Vence. No doubt she would tell her mom, Maria, what had occurred, and his mother, Kelly, as well. This was a lover's quarrel that ended without resolution. Once both women knew of the situation, they, too, would be terrified about what might happen to him.

He dressed in a light blue short-sleeved shirt, navy shorts and loafers. He headed to the hotel café even though food didn't seem appealing. Without Danielle by his side, he felt as if someone ripped off his arm. The lack of her smile and her presence hurt in the center of his chest. The café smelled of fresh bakery goods, roast coffee and bacon. He selected a small plate of scrambled eggs and potatoes from the buffet line and chose a table close to the open doors on the balcony. Once seated, he motioned for the waitress to pour him some coffee, hoping it was very strong, as most European coffee tended to be. Sitting with his back to the sun, it warmed him and helped relax his tense neck muscles. Part of him wanted to get on the next plane and fly home; another part of him, the cop he was before he became a successful artist, was determined to find out if the person Danielle saw was Ryan or, in fact, was someone else. He sipped the black coffee trying to concoct a plan.

It made no sense to call the hotel to talk to the woman, Cassandra, and ask the same questions. By now, she'd be very suspicious of two people asking about someone named Ryan Coltrane. If he was working there, most likely he'd be ending his shift late in the afternoon. How would he approach him? When Danielle saw him at the construction site, odds were he saw her too, but maybe not. Perhaps he was busy. He finished his breakfast and decided to stop at a gun store and a camera shop as well. A camera with a long telephoto lens would be needed for a stakeout. There was considerable shrubbery with tall pine and pistachio trees at the construction site where he could hide out later in the day. Hopefully he'd catch a glimpse of the person Danielle saw.

He fingered his wallet for a business card. Another possibility would be to find out who the site manager was, give them a business card and pretend he was hoping to sell some of his large art pieces. Although that was a possibility, if he met with someone to discuss his art, it would be awkward to be glancing around looking at workers at the same time. There was no guarantee they wanted or needed any art, and should they say "no thanks" he'd have to be on his way. If he spotted Ryan and Ryan saw him, he was certain Ryan would flee. He was no longer a cop so he had no jurisdiction in Mallorca. Not much he could do. Chasing Ryan on foot up and down the treacherous mountain terrain until he caught him made no sense at all. It would end in a knock-down drag-out fight because Ryan wouldn't surrender.

Although he wanted justice for his little sister, he wanted to do it the right way. That meant he'd have to involve the Mallorca police. Before he could arrest Ryan, assuming it was Ryan, he'd have to know it was him for sure, then have the police arrest him. Also, he wasn't sure what the extradition laws were in Mallorca about getting Ryan back to Nice. He'd have to explore that option with the police.

At the camera shop, he bought a high-powered Nikon camera, a telephoto lens and a pair of binoculars. It was impossible to purchase a gun, even though he tried to convince the salesclerk that his hotel room had been robbed and he didn't feel safe. For now, he'd drive around the island, tour some art galleries, and take a swim later at the hotel— anything to pass time until he'd change clothes into a dark t-shirt and cargo pants for camouflage to hide out in the woods. The red rental car was way too visible, so he decided to rent a moped and a helmet.

CHAPTER 16
Danielle

Danielle cried most of the way home to St. Paul-de-Vence on the plane, to the point where the stewardess asked her if she could help in some way. It was a bumpy, short flight, and she was glad to be home. Marie, her mother, was waiting for her at the airport. She spotted her mother in the airport lounge.

Marie took one look at Danielle and knew this was her sensitive daughter in the middle of a catastrophe. Her face was flushed, eyes red and swollen, nose blotchy—a face she had seen before Evan and Danielle were married and had a fight. "Aww, sweetie, what happened?" Marie hugged her daughter and rubbed the small of her back.

"I made a mess out of something," Danielle met her mother's gaze.

"You can tell me all about it on the way home."

They walked to the luggage arrival and waited for Danielle's suitcase.

"You hungry?" Marie asked.

"Not at all." Danielle winced.

"I'll fix you something when we get home. I know when you aren't hungry, something really is wrong."

"How's Trevor?" Danielle asked. "I missed him so much."

"He's fine, honey. The most adorable, good boy."

Danielle's suitcase arrived on the turnstile. Marie grabbed it for her and they began to walk to the car. "Do you want to go home first, or come home with me?"

"I want to see Trevor and we can talk, and then I'll take him home. Is Kelly still at the house?"

"Yes. She's watching Trevor."

"How's Chloe and Lena? I've missed my sisters."

"Chloe is on hospital shift four days a week, and three days off, so that's a better schedule for her. Lena's in love with her boyfriend and enjoys her interior design work.

"And Dad?"

"He's fine. Busy as ever with the yachting business. Plenty of clients."

"I'm looking forward to seeing Amber and Juliette, my youngest sisters are growing so fast, and my brothers, Lucas, Josh and dear Valentin, that sweet, dyslexic sibling of mine. It's hard to believe he's nearly nine year's old. I'm so happy he's reading well. For a long time, we didn't think he'd be able to sort out letters, but working with him helped a great deal. Now he reads *Harry Potter* on his own and has a real love for books."

"Lucas's lavender business still going well?" Danielle asked.

"Yes. Busy time of the year. He works too hard, you know."

Danielle nodded and smiled at her mother, her French heritage evident by her accent. Even though Marie grew up in the United States, and was bilingual, she preferred speaking English. Danielle was pleased she resembled her mother—a snapshot of what she would look like as she aged—the same facial bone structure, the freckles, the thick auburn hair turned up into a French twist.

They drove in silence from the Nice airport to St. Paul-de-Vence, through bougainvillea-lined streets, framed by tall graceful palm trees, and flowering bushes along the azure Mediterranean. It was a balmy day with soft breezes, puffy billowing clouds and warm temperatures. Danielle felt oddly displaced without Evan, and already regretted her decision to come home. Marie arrived at the palatial estate's entry gate, pushed in the security code and drove up the winding tree-lined driveway. Thor, their large black and tan Alsatian Shepherd, started barking until he recognized Danielle, then ran to her nuzzling into her legs. "Looks like he missed you," Marie said. Danielle bent down to hug Thor and let him lick her face with happy wet kisses. They walked past the kitchen into the immense living room where Evan's mom sat on one of the two sofas watching Trevor asleep in a playpen. Although Danielle wanted to pick up Trevor, she didn't want to wake him. "Hi, Kelly. Thanks for watching Trevor. Was he a good boy?"

"The best. I adore that boy," Kelly smiled. Danielle and Kelly hugged, and Danielle sat down on the sofa opposite her trying to relax knowing an inquisition was about to start.

"Want something to drink?" Marie asked.

"Got some of your homemade ice tea?"

"Sure. I'll get it from the refrigerator." Marie left the room and headed into the kitchen.

Kelly stared at Danielle and prodded with grave concern in her voice. "So, my dear, what happened? Is Evan with you?"

"No, Evan's still in Mallorca. I did something really stupid—I'll explain when Mama's in the room."

Marie returned with a pitcher of ice tea and a tray of oatmeal cookies. "Here's some fresh lemons and sugar if it's not sweet enough."

Marie sat down next to Danielle, took a sip of tea and placed the glass on the coffee table. She sighed while putting her hands on her lap, anxious to hear why Danielle came home alone.

Danielle took a deep breath and unfolded the story. Both women let her finish without overt criticism or judgment. Since Danielle was Marie's daughter, Kelly kept quiet and let Marie take the lead.

"I was really sure Ryan was dead," Marie said. "We wanted it to be so."

"I can understand why you panicked, but you did so without really knowing if the person you saw was Ryan, or someone who just looked like him," Marie noted, her face contorted in a quandary of surprise and dismay.

Danielle's face flushed. She momentarily sat there and hung her head in embarrassment. She glanced up, struggling for words. "I'm sorry, Mama. I couldn't stay there and let Evan pursue this nightmare. I couldn't give him an ultimatum. I didn't want to say that he had to choose between Ryan or me, because I knew that would be putting him in an impossible situation. If I waited until morning, he probably wouldn't have let me leave, but the wall between us would have been impossible to resolve. I left him a note saying I was here waiting." Tears ran down her face and she used her fingers to wipe them away.

"Are you sure it was Ryan that you saw?" Marie asked.

"No. I'm not sure. The shock of seeing Ryan was awful— my mind went blank. I felt weak and dizzy. I thought I was going to faint."

"So, Evan never saw him?" Kelly asked.

"No, he was looking in a different direction. I panicked and asked to be taken to the car. Apparently, I was white as a sheet."

"What do you think Evan will do?" Marie put her hand on her daughter's shoulder.

"I'm fairly certain he'll find a way to confront Ryan to see for himself, but he'll probably involve the Mallorca police. Evan's mindset is being a cop; he's not thinking like an artist right now. He'll do what he has to do. No matter what the cost, he's determined to bring justice for Ashley's death."

"I don't think you should have left him there. You're his wife. Couples work out their differences," Kelly said, aware that she was preaching.

Danielle met her gaze. "If something happened to Evan, I'd be raising Trevor alone. I couldn't live with that fear. I don't want to be a widow."

Kelly wiped her brow. "Well, we are all terrified now. What do we do?"

Marie offered, "I'll talk to Gaspard when he gets home. He knows what Evan went through when Ryan blew up his yacht, not to mention how he put Lena in danger. It was an awful time."

"I really should be going back home," Kelly said and rose from the sofa. I can get a flight out first thing in the morning. Promise me, Danielle, that you two will work this out."

Danielle nodded and bit the inside of her cheek knowing this was not going to be an easy situation.

The front door opened. Gaspard entered the room.

"Danielle, what are you doing home so early? I thought your honeymoon was supposed to be three weeks."

"It's a long story, Dad, but I'll fill you in," Danielle said. "Have a seat."

Gaspard walked to the sofa where his daughter was sitting, and sat down next to her sensing something was very wrong. "So, honey, tell me what happened?"

She bit her upper lip and explained the story again to her father, each time telling the details that made her stomach turn. Gaspard said, "Maybe Evan will decide this goose chase is not worth the risk of losing you or putting himself in so much danger."

Gaspard added, "I have to say I'm distraught to learn that Ryan might be alive. Even if we couldn't prove he died when he blew up his yacht, we saw the explosion debris. There was no body, so we all wished it to be true that he was either dead or assumed if he escaped, we'd never see him again. Someone could have picked him up from the water knowing where he'd be. In order to escape the explosion, he would have left the yacht long before he blew it up. I'm just as vested in this disaster, not only because of the death of Evan's sister, Ashley, but because Ryan killed Armond, my trusted controller. There was no justice for that death either, but we needed to believe in Ryan's death. If it's not true, then Evan will want to bring him in to the police. Won't he have to first prove the person you saw was actually Ryan?"

"Yes, Dad. There is the possibility the person I saw was someone else."

"I'll call Evan," Gaspard said. "I have his cell number. Maybe there is something I can do to help."

"Thanks, Dad." Danielle leaned over and gave her father a hug.

Trevor woke up with a huge yawn, and Danielle picked him up. "Hi, sweetie. How's my big boy?"

He clapped his hands together in excitement and held his wiggling fingers toward her to be picked up. The scent of Trevor's skin cradled to her neck was a soothing balm. She sighed, and held him tightly—a comfort she desperately needed.

CHAPTER 17
Nick

Nick woke up to a cacophony of commotion. He peered out of his stateroom portal and noticed several cops running yellow crime tape in front of Chad's boat. What the hell? He quickly dressed in shorts and yesterday's t-shirt, slipped his feet into his flip-flops, walked through the galley and headed toward Chad's boat. As he approached, a tall policeman with slightly grey hair and a square jaw held up his hand and said he couldn't go further.

Nick ran his fingers through his unruly hair placing it behind his ears. "Can you tell me what happened?"

"I'm Officer Lopez. This is a murder scene. Apparently, someone bashed in his head with a baseball bat. Did you know the victim?"

"Yes, but not well. When did this happen?"

"We're not sure. Sometime during the night. Medical Examiner said the body's been cold about six hours. I've been checking with other boats docked here and residents living in the marina. Did you hear anything?"

Nick shook his head. "No, I get migraines and take medication. It knocks me out for hours. This all happened last night?"

"Around 2:00 this morning according to the coroner."

A portly woman with her red hair in a frizzy mess atop her head approached them. "I think you ought to talk to this man right here pointing at Nick. They were always fighting about noise. Yelling actually, to where we could not sleep because of the commotion." The woman stood with her hands on her hips, her lips pursed in an accusatory manner.

Television cameras were already on the scene. Bystanders were numb and noisy, dismayed at having a murder in their locale.

Another thin, tight-lipped short female officer was writing all this down. She turned to the frizzy-haired woman. "And your name is?"

"Mrs. Delmonico. I live on the boat in the slip across the pier," she said while poking a finger at Nick's chest. "I've seen you on Chad's boat."

"That so?" Officer Lopez asked with raised eyebrows.

Nick's mind started spinning nervously. "I don't even know the guy well. I was over there for drinks once. That was it."

Officer Lopez motioned for the female officer to join them. "This is Officer Cortina, and you are?"

"Uh, Nick Fontaine." He nervously picked the inside of his thumb.

"When were you on Chad's boat?" Officer Lopez asked.

Nick shrugged his shoulders. "A couple of nights ago. I can't remember exactly."

"We'll want to talk to people in this marina who might I've heard something," Officer Cortina said, then started writing notes on a small pad.

Nick glanced up in time to see the baseball bat being lowered into a large plastic bag. In a split recollection he knew he'd touched that bat. Good Lord, his fingerprints were on it, but he deduced other fingerprints most likely were on the bat as well. Who would have wanted to kill Chad? Seemed like a nice enough guy.

A gurney was wheeled onto the pier. Several policemen carried Chad's body and lifted him onto the gurney. An arm dropped over the side. Nick gasped when he saw the amount of blood on Chad's head, his face hardly recognizable. The coroner placed a white sheet over the victim and they wheeled him down the pier past gawking onlookers.

Nick started pacing. "I need to get going."

"Which is your boat?" Officer Lopez asked.

Nick pointed to his boat. "I have to get to work."

Officer Cortina asked, "Where do you work?"

"I'm the construction foreman at *Cielo*...the new hotel being built."

"We'll want to talk to you this evening. We're sending what we found to forensics."

"Mrs. Delmonico, we'll want to interview you as well. Will you be on your boat this evening?" Officer Lopez said.

"Yeah, sure. Our boat's that one over there—the one with the blue stripe on the hull. My husband and I will be home."

Nick turned and walked back to his boat, his knees feeling unsteady. How could a crime take place right next to his boat? What would happen when the cops started digging into his background? He felt like the walls were closing in. First Danielle shows up on the island, and now his boat neighbor is killed with a baseball bat carrying his fingerprints. He reached into his nightstand and took the bottle of migraine pills, set it on the bed, dropped his clothes and headed into the shower. He'd be late for work and would have to explain to Cassandra what had occurred—a murder, no less. What else could go wrong?

CHAPTER 18
Danielle

No sooner had Kelly retired for the evening when Chloe in her hospital scrubs walked into the living room and noticed Danielle sitting alone on the terrace. "Hey sis, what are you doing here?"

"Better sit down, Chloe. It's a long story."

"Is Evan here?" Chloe asked, her face registering dismay.

"No, he's still in Mallorca." Danielle frowned while gently bouncing Trevor on her knee.

"What in the world happened?" Chloe asked.

"We had taken a ride up the mountain to a new hotel construction site on the island. I thought I saw Ryan in a group of workers."

"You what?"

"I know, same build, same face, really sun-bleached blond hair. I couldn't have been more than thirty feet from him. He was talking to some men, as if he was working at the construction site."

"Are you sure it was Ryan?"

"No, I'm not positive. My mind could have played tricks, but unless Ryan has a double, which is possible, it really seemed like him."

Chloe asked, "Wasn't Evan with you?"

"Yes, but he was looking in a different direction. By the time he looked toward the men in that group, Ryan had turned away."

"Did you say something?"

"Danielle shook her head. "I should have, but my mind went blank. I think I was in shock. Evan said I turned ashen. He assumed I had eaten too much earlier, then hiking up the hill in higher altitude made me feel faint."

Knowing Evan, he'd be back to being a cop. He'd want to confront Ryan or whoever this person is, then determine for himself what to do."

Chloe's eyes opened wide. "Aren't you afraid of what might happen to him?"

"Of, course, I'm terrified Evan is going to get killed."

Chloe sat quietly for a few minutes pondering what her sister had just told her. "Can't Evan go to the police?"

Danielle turned toward her sister. "He could, but the police have no jurisdiction. It's not like Evan's a Federal Marshall where he could extradite Ryan back here to Nice for Armond's murder. Don't forget that the newspaper article that came out after the explosion said Ryan had died. For all intents and purposes, Ryan *is* dead.

"This is mind-boggling," Chloe said, turned and took her sister's free hand in hers. "I don't think you should have left, but maybe Evan will follow you home and he won't pursue Ryan. He loves you so much—you both waited some eight months after Trevor was born to take a belated honeymoon. Now that you left, Evan has to be in shock. He'll probably be angry."

Danielle turned toward her sister. "He was already very angry with me because of a stupid phone call I made to the hotel. He feels I blew his cover—his chance to decide on his own how he wanted to handle this."

"I agree with him. You shouldn't have made that call," Chloe said shaking her head, then reached over and took Trevor to her lap. He gurgled, giggled and wiggled and placed his arms around Chloe's neck.

The front door slammed and Lucas entered, his briefcase in one hand and his jacket in the other. He glanced out the living room French doors and saw Danielle.

"Hey, sis. What are you doing home? I thought your honeymoon was for another couple of weeks?"

Danielle got up to hug Lucas. "You'd better sit down. You're not going to believe what's happened."

Lucas tossed his jacket on a lawn chair and set his briefcase on the patio. His face registered concern as he sat down on a chaise cushion.

Danielle reiterated the story as Lucas shook his head in dismay.

"What does Dad think?" Lucas asked, his blue eyes squinting with apprehension.

"Dad's going to call Evan on his cell later. Maybe he can convince him not to pursue this, but I doubt it."

Danielle, Chloe and Lucas sat in silence, watching the Mediterranean sunset in the distance unable to come up with anything else to say to each other.

"Do you want anything to drink?" Marie said as she entered the terrace.

Danielle said she wanted a glass of white wine, Chloe asked for a Bordeaux. Lucas sighed and said he wanted a scotch straight up.

CHAPTER 19
Nick

Nick rode his motorcycle to work and thought about what he might say to Cassie when he got to the office. Traffic was heavy and it took him longer than the usual forty minutes to get to *Cielo*. No doubt the murder would be on the evening news. He couldn't stay late to do any journal entries because the cops wanted to talk to him. The air was muggy and abnormally humid for this time of year, even more so because of the recent storm that passed. He sweated under his helmet with droplets of water cascading down his face and back. Telling Cassie about the murder seemed the right thing to do, but he didn't feel he needed to tell her about the baseball bat with his fingerprints on it. He sped up around a slow-moving truck and wove back into traffic.

Arriving at the hotel, he parked his cycle in the newly finished parking lot which curved around the hotel's entrance.

He took a deep breath, twisted the long hair at his neck with a rubber band he'd kept on his wrist and headed to the construction trailer. He opened the trailer door and ran into Cassie coming out.

"You're late," she said looking at her watch.

"I know. Do you have a few minutes? I've a lot to tell you."

"Okay," she nodded, turned and walked back into the trailer. She sat in a chair adjacent to his desk with a blank expression on her face.

"There was a murder last night in the marina."

"What?" She gasped.

"Boat next to mine. Old guy had me over for drinks once. Used to keep his TV on so loud at night I couldn't sleep."

"Do they know who did it?" she said.

"Not yet. I ran into two cops at the crime scene. People were gathered at the marina, gawking, wondering—other boat owners were milling around in shock. TV cameras were already covering the scene."

"That's so awful. What does that have to do with you?"

"Nothing. I had been to the guy's boat once for drinks. I barely knew him."

"What was his name?"

"Chad Callahan. Nice enough guy from Northern Ireland. Cops want to talk to me, and other boat owners later to see if any of us heard or saw something. I can't stay late tonight, and I'm sorry I didn't call about being late this morning—I was dumbfounded."

"Do you know how he died?"

"Someone beat him up pretty badly."

"So, he wasn't shot?"

Nick shook his head. "No." He fingered the migraine pills in his pocket.

"There isn't much crime on this island, but enough so that it makes me nervous to think of it as an unsafe place. Like many other cities, there is organized crime here too," she said.

Desperate to change the subject, he said, "Understood. What's the status of progress on the hotel?"

"They're laying the subfloor today, then the marble for the entry. If any bad pieces show up, tell them to scrap those and use only quality cuts for the entry."

"Will do. I think the entrance to the hotel looks awesome now with the curved arch and hand-painted Spanish tiles inset all around the curved arch. Very classy."

She smiled. "I'm glad you appreciate the architecture. I wanted this hotel to resemble a Spanish villa and that's why I chose decorative elements more like someone's home than a hotel."

"You have great taste."

"That's nice of you to say, Nick. I'm going to check on progress. Why don't you come with me? Take a pad of paper along to note any problems needing correction."

"Sounds good." He picked up a pad of paper and followed her up the cobblestone path to the hotel.

He was glad the hotel was nearing completion. He'd seen a lot of progress on the hotel since he started working for Cassie. The stucco on the outside of the building was a honey-colored two-tone application. Corinthian columns were placed on each side of the front portico which sported a groin-vaulted ceiling stenciled in scrolls and acanthus leaves. Nick said, "I like these enormous coach lights that flank each side of the etched glass doors reminiscent of old-world Spain. Cassie said, "I wanted them to be impressive and had them specially made."

They continued walking, observing minor issues needing attention. Her hand brushed his as they walked. He wanted to hold her hand, but it wasn't appropriate. They went through the front doors and looked at the interior which was vast and yet charming. The trusses were exposed in the entry, giving it a grand statement of rustic luxury. Wrought-iron chandeliers hung from the ceiling between the beams. To the right was a registration desk with granite counters in blue Bahia. A concierge station had a waterfall streaming in the background from the first-floor ceiling down to the spa center, an architectural feature she and her father had designed for peace and tranquility. "Stunning," Nick said. Several clerestory windows cast rays of sun across the two-story mezzanine. They continued walking together admiring the quality work.

While they walked, Nick momentarily forgot his fears—the fears that would consume him when he stopped working—fears about Evan Wentworth being on this island—fears about Chad being murdered and what that investigation into his background would mean this evening—fears about what the police might uncover about his background. He bit the inside of his cheek until he drew blood, a bad habit he had since childhood, sucked it down and continued his walk with Cassie. As long as he was inside the hotel, he couldn't be seen by Evan's prying eyes if he was to show up.

He took a deep breath and tried to concentrate on his job, a job he actually enjoyed. Cassie was a good boss, very attractive with her dark skin and ebony hair, intelligent and competent. Had she not been his boss, he would have liked to get to know her better, perhaps even try to date her, but that was not to be.

She was friendly, but her demeanor was that of a boss and him as the subordinate, which he respected. Getting laid was not on his mind. Staying under the radar and not getting caught as 'Ryan Coltrane' was the first and last thing he thought of every night before he went to sleep. The entire persona of Nick Fontaine had become real to him—a new job he enjoyed, a luxury boat needing some repairs but moored in a beautiful marina, clean air and beauty everywhere he looked—a life he wanted to keep that seemed to be slipping through his fingers.

CHAPTER 20
Evan

Evan rode his moped cautiously up the winding road to the hotel *Cielo*. He was surprised how much traffic there was, cars weaving in and out of a two-lane road, drivers always rushing as if they'd run out of minutes. He had put his camera, telephoto lens and tripod in the moped's basket. It rattled around as he drove the serpentine road. The weather was humid without a breeze. Cumulus clouds tumbled in the sky resembling mountains of another dimension—a place Evan looked homeward to where heaven might be. He missed Danielle more than life itself right now, but finding out if the person she saw was Ryan was something he had to do.

His cell phone pinged and thinking it might be Danielle, he pulled over to the side of the road to answer the call. Instead, it was Gaspard.

He pulled over to the side of the road to answer the call.

"Gaspard, what's up?"

"Danielle told us what happened. I'm heartsick about how she feels, but I understand you were first and foremost a cop and will always be a cop.

"We went through so much with Ryan," Evan said. "If this *is* Ryan, then I have to find out for myself. I'm on my way right now to the hotel where Danielle saw him."

"Be careful, son. This man, if he *is* Ryan, is a murderer. If I were there and saw him, I'd kill him myself for what he did to Lena."

"Understood." Evan said.

"What's your plan?

"I bought binoculars, a high-powered camera, and a telephoto lens. I'm hoping I can spot Ryan leaving work."

"So, where will you do the stakeout?"

"On the side of the hill in a heavily forested area overlooking the parking lot. There are some massive rock outcroppings up there. I have dark slacks, and a baseball cap for camouflage. The sun is going down already, and if I could watch the workers leaving the hotel, I might spot him."

"Good luck with that. But if you do, then what?"

"I don't know yet. If I see him, and know for sure it's Ryan, I'll contact Sheriff Cosley in El Dorado Hills to see if it's a case we can reopen, or if I need to contact the local police and do an extradition back to Nice. Because the murder was committed in Nice, I wouldn't be extraditing him to El Dorado Hills—he'd have to go down for the murder of Armond—I don't care which murder he pays for, as long as I have justice for Ashley and Armond."

"I understand. Keep me informed. Please be careful," Gaspard said.

"I will."

Gaspard said, "You know Danielle's devastated?"

"I do. I'm sorry for what I'm putting her through. If it is Ryan, I can't let this go. I love Danielle so deeply. Tell her I'm sorry I yelled at her, but Ryan has been a thorn between us for a long time. I owe it to her to end this once and for all."

"Okay. Be safe. Remember, he's a killer without a conscience."

"Don't I know it."

Gaspard hung up. Evan sat there on his moped feeling a shroud of grief engulf him again. Just talking about Ryan brought back memories of Ashley—caught in the crossfire of a bank robbery at such a young age—a robbery where other people died as well. Evan had never forgiven himself for having her in his squad car that day. They had gone to Starbucks. When the bank robbery broke out, gunshots were fired and one of the stray bullets struck Ashley. She had clung to life for a short time and then died at the hospital—a day like no other, and a lifetime of guilt through his own fault. It was an accident, and yes, he was off-duty, but if she hadn't been with him on the fateful day, she'd still be alive. With every breath he took, he regretted that nightmare and missed her every day of his life.

Evan leaned into the turn and spotted the hotel through the trees. The brilliant sun was setting, the sky ablaze with pink, gold and violet ribbons. A steady breeze shifted palm fronds and olive tree branches back and forth. He avoided the parking lot—too obvious, and instead, as planned, nestled into the rocks and shrubbery on the side of the road. He waited until there were no cars coming or going, so no one would see him leave the road. Dismounting from his moped, he hauled it into the brush and laid it down next to an outcropping of rocks. He opened the basket flap and took out his equipment. One large boulder was about waist high and somewhat flat— a surface that would do just fine to set up a tri-pod stand.

His throat was parched from the ride. He guzzled down water which he brought along assuming he would be at this stakeout for some time. With the sun down, the temperature quickly cooled. He removed his sunglasses and turned his baseball cap backwards. If he bent over the rock with his camera equipment he'd be in a somewhat crouched stance, but it would do. He quickly set up the tripod, attached the high-powered telephoto lens to his camera and focused on the parking lot with his binoculars. To his surprise, the parking lot was full—at least thirty cars or more, several jeeps and a few motorcycles. As workers left, he hoped to spot their faces from the driver's side. His legs tired from his awkward stance so he sat down in the dirt waiting for workers to leave the hotel. He could hear crickets and various birds chirping. The wind started to pick up, so much so that he needed to hold on to the tripod. The telephoto lens was heavy and tended to sway in the breeze unless he held it still. This was more difficult than he imagined.

He began to hear engines of cars starting to leave the work site. He steadied his camera, had a good view of the driver's side of the cars, but as workers left he didn't recognize anyone. Many were local Catalan residents—clearly not Ryan. He adjusted the focus, impatient for what he hoped to see. Most of the cars, jeeps and motorcycles had left the parking lot. How many men were working at the hotel? More than he expected. He adjusted his binoculars and saw a blond-haired guy with a man-bun walk to his motorcycle. Could that be Ryan? He clicked several frames in a row, but soon lost the image when the man put on a helmet. He'd study the film for a closeup after he had it developed.

Then he felt it before he saw it—something slithered across the back of his calves. He didn't dare move, because intuitively he knew it was a large snake. It never occurred to him that snakes were on the island. After all, snakes weren't in Hawaii, so why would there be snakes on Mallorca? He held his breath and tried not to flinch. His legs cramped. The snake crawled over the back of his calf and coiled around his shoe. If it were poisonous, he'd dared not make a move. The thought of dying by a snake bite crossed his mind. He didn't breathe.

A gust of wind knocked over the poorly placed small tripod and camera, the telephoto lens toppled into the brush and the snake uncoiled and slithered into the underbrush. It didn't occur to him to bring a flashlight, and he didn't want to reach down in the tall grass to grope for the camera equipment for fear he'd get bitten by the snake. Thankfully, he remembered the flashlight on his iPhone. Another car was leaving the parking lot. He couldn't find the camera and was annoyed he didn't get a shot. Damn. This didn't turn out as expected. After the car left, he turned on his phone's flashlight and spotted the camera and tripod. The snake was still moving in the dirt, so he took a cell phone photo of it. He packed up his camera equipment, turned his baseball cap around and lifted his moped off the ground. Couldn't get out of there fast enough. Gave him the chills. Maybe there was a den of snakes where he was crouched—panic swept over him. He pushed the moped back to the road, started the engine and got the hell out of there.

Riding down the mountains of the Tramuntana calmed his rattled nerves. He took the hairpin turns slowly, cars honking their horns impatiently for him to get out of the way or go faster, which he couldn't do on a two-lane road with no shoulder. It seemed like a half-hour before he got to the hotel *Calatrava*. He needed a drink, but first he parked the moped, gathered up his camera equipment and headed up to his room.

He slid the room key into the door, walked into his room and turned on the lights and put his camera equipment on a chair. How very lonely the hotel room felt without Danielle. It was almost as if he'd never met her—what his life would be like without her. The silence was overwhelming. After a quick shower, a stiff drink and a half-eaten sandwich waiting in the mini-bar, he thought about going to sleep.

He turned on the TV for background noise with the nightly news because he couldn't stand the quiet without someone to talk to. First thing in the morning he'd have to find a shop that could develop his camera film. Curious about the snake, he Googled snakes on Mallorca and found a match to the photo he had taken. A Horseshoe Whip Snake, of all creatures, was not native to the island, but came over on trees imported from the peninsula. Snakes tended to seek out cool places, and it made sense to him that it was cooler up the mountain around the hotel construction site area. He was thankful the snake was not poisonous—a small comfort when fear alone was enough to kill someone.

Evan desperately missed Danielle—her perfume, her laughter, her soft skin, her passionate kisses. What had he done to their relationship? He'd call her in the morning and tell her how much he loved her.

CHAPTER 21
Evan

The bedroom terrace door slammed into the wall jolting Evan awake. He sat up, rubbed his eyes and glanced at the clock. He was surprised he'd slept so soundly, courtesy of the scotch he downed, but he had a mild headache he hoped would disappear with a quick shower. Fumbling for his shoes under the bed, he set his loafers aside and hit the TV remote, then closed the terrace door before another guest of wind would slam it shut. He ambled into the bathroom, turned on the shower and welcomed the sudsy soap and warm water.

For a few minutes he forgot about his problems, but he still had a hollow ache in his chest because Danielle wasn't there. Little things one took for granted like a good morning kiss, watching her brush her teeth with her auburn hair piled into a ponytail, their hugs and pleasant routine of getting dressed together. Simple things he wasn't experiencing. He dried off with a huge fluffy towel and listened to the TV in the background—something about a murder in the marina, a man named Chadwick Callahan, an assumed name, formerly with the Real Irish Republican Army—a fugitive wanted for many years who escaped from Northern Ireland and was hiding out on his boat in the marina. The announcer said, '*On August 15, 1998 bombers intended to blow up the courthouse in Omagh, County Tyrone with a 300 lb. bomb but could not find a parking space, so they had parked very close to the courthouse. They cordoned off the street to keep civilians out of the area, but inadvertently backed the crowd closer to the bomb which exploded killing twenty-nine people and injuring two-hundred-twenty others. Apparently, they never caught the bomber until now, hiding out on his sailboat in Mallorca with a huge stash of currency.*'

Evan brushed his teeth while watching TV, thinking it was unbelievable how many criminals changed identities and went on with other lives as if the identity they left behind didn't exist. He wondered, if Ryan was alive, how he managed to overlook his past as if the terrible things he had done hadn't happened. No conscience, no regrets. He watched the TV announcer talking to marina residents and was about to head back into the bathroom when he spotted a tall blonde man with his back to the camera talking to one of the policemen. The man was about the same build as Ryan. The cop was also talking to a woman. Evan wished he could see the blond man's face, but he couldn't. It occurred to him that he was being paranoid—people were beginning to look like Ryan when most likely they were anyone but him. Evan finished with his teeth, went back into the bathroom to rinse and managed to miss the blond-haired man's face on camera. Evan decided to take a run later in the day to shake off his recriminations. For now, he wanted to get dressed and have his film developed.

Before he went to the camera shop he needed to talk to Danielle to apologize. He called her on her cell phone. It rang three times and went into voice mail. Dejected, he left her a message to please call him so they could talk, and that he was sorry he was so tough with her, but most of all, that he loved her very much. He then called Sheriff Cosley, his former boss in El Dorado Hills, California.

"Hey, Bob, it's Evan."

"Nice to hear from you, Evan, What's up?"

"I need your help."

Bob chuckled. "You want me to visit you again in St. Paul?"

"No. I'm not in St. Paul, I'm in Mallorca on a belated honeymoon vacation that isn't going very well."

"Speechless here. I don't know what to say about your honeymoon not working out. Didn't you and Danielle get married quite a long time ago?"

"Yes, we did, but delayed the honeymoon because of the baby."

"Oh, that's right. I forgot she was pregnant. How is the baby?"

"Trevor's a rambunctious toddler who makes life worth living." Evan turned off the TV and sat down on the bed. "I hated to call, Bob, but something has come up here that I couldn't have imagined."

"Okay, you have my interest." Bob said.

"Danielle and I were checking out the sights on the island and we stopped at a construction site for a new hotel. She thought she saw Ryan standing with a group of people."

"You mean Ryan Coltrane?"

"Can you believe it?"

"Did you see him?" Bob asked.

"No, I was looking in a different direction."

"Didn't Danielle tell you she saw him?"

"No, not right away. She was in shock and wasn't completely sure it was Ryan.

"Well, we were never sure he blew up his yacht and killed himself—we just didn't know where he went after the explosion. We assumed he survived it because we never found a body," Bob said.

Evan swallowed air before speaking. "What I want to know is whether we can reopen this case."

"No, Evan. I put out a press release to give some closure to those who lost their lives in the robbery, including your sister, Ashley. The police in Nice put out a newspaper story after the accident stating that he was dead. I'm not bringing a dead man back to life—that case is closed. I doubt if you could get the Nice police to reopen the case either. If Ryan has really resurfaced, he'd have to be brought up on some new charge."

"Yeah, I was afraid of that."

"Do you know where this guy is you think is Ryan?"

Evan cleared his throat. "He may be working for the new hotel that's going up—doing what, I can't imagine."

"Doesn't sound likely to me. Can't you let this go? I mean, you don't even know the guy Danielle saw is, in fact, Ryan. It could be someone else."

"But what if it isn't?"

"That's a tough one," Bob said. "If it turns out it is Ryan, he probably has a different identity. He's smart, remember?"

"I can't forget about this, even though I know I should. But he was responsible for Ashley's death and if it's Ryan, then she deserves justice."

"Understood, but remember, he's killed before, and there is no one he would rather see dead than you, Evan. By the way, how is Danielle handling all of this?"

Evan sighed. "Not well. We had a tiff and she went home. She called the new hotel to ask about Ryan working there while I was out getting a replacement rental car."

"That was bold on her part." Bob stated.

"I know. I was miffed at the time because I wanted to control the situation."

"Well, I hope you work things out, Evan."

"Thanks for your help, Bob. This may be a wild goose chase, but until I find out if this guy really is Ryan, I can't rest."

"You have a gun?"

Evan swallowed, "No, but I'm not stupid either. I'll get Danielle to send it to me along with my Federal Firearms License and work clothes."

"Be safe. Patch things up with Danielle. She's one beautiful woman."

Evan sighed. "Will do." He disconnected his phone. The conversation left him feeling as if he needed to run a marathon.

After he made a trip to the camera shop to see about getting his film developed, he decided he would go for a much-needed run from the hotel to the marina. Running always calmed him down, gave him better clarity, better insight. His phone pinged. Danielle had tried to call him while he was talking to Bob. Drats.

CHAPTER 22
Evan and Danielle

Evan quickly dialed Danielle's cell phone and sat on the edge of the bed feeling his nerves twitch.

"Danielle?" "Did I catch you at a bad time?"

"No, I was just putting Trevor down for a nap. I tried to reach you."

"I was talking to Sheriff Cosley because I needed his help."

"What can Bob do? He's in California."

"It's frustrating. Because of the press release put out last year about Ryan Coltrane's death, that cold case was closed for those people killed in the bank robbery. There's nothing he can do to reopen the case, because we declared Ryan dead."

Danielle sighed. "I understand. How are you Evan? Are you still angry with me?

"No, of course not. I'm miserable that you left and went home, but I deserved that. I'm really sorry I was so harsh with you. Please forgive me. I know you wanted to protect me, and that if this guy wasn't really Ryan, you felt we could have ended the drama right there."

"Yes, I had hoped he was anyone but Ryan. What did you find out?"

"Not much. I bought a high-powered camera and telephoto lens to try to capture him leaving work, but haven't had the film developed yet.

"Where did you go to take the photos?"

"Near the construction site, hidden in the bushes so I could see the parking lot and watch workers leave."

Danielle cleared her throat and asked, "Did you see him?"

"Not sure. Once the film is developed, we'll see if I have a good shot or not. One guy who might have been him was getting on a motorcycle, then put on a helmet and I really didn't get a good look at him."

"Evan, I am so worried about you. Hopefully you understand why I couldn't have stayed there—I would have been in your way. I didn't want to criticize the way you felt you should handle this."

"I promise if the photos don't look like Ryan, I will drop this and come home."

Danielle sighed. "There's nothing I want more."

Evan tried to change the subject. "How's my big boy?"

"Darling as ever. He was so thrilled to see me. Your mom did a great job baby-sitting for us. She gets along so well with Marie. Those two grandmothers were in their element while we were gone."

"Was my mother upset with you for coming home early?"

"I think both of our mothers were floored that I came home without you; I give Kelly credit for not preaching to me about not staying with you. Obviously, she's very concerned. She's worried about your safety. My Dad said he would call you. Did he?"

"Yes. We had a good talk. He doesn't want Ryan coming between us, but understands my need to end this with justice once and for all. I'll keep you informed," Evan said.

"Promise me you'll call me every night so that I know you're safe."

"Scouts honor. I promise. I love you, Danielle, and I would never do anything on purpose to hurt you."

Danielle could feel her eyes watering and words catching in her throat.

"I love you, Evan. You're the air that I breathe, the sun that shines in my heart, and the man who is the father of our son, our most precious gift from God. Please be careful."

"I promise. I'll talk to you tomorrow night."

Evan hung up the phone and felt the emptiness in the air slice through his consciousness. Without Danielle, he felt as if a limb was missing. As much as he craved justice for Ashley, he hoped the person Danielle saw was anyone but Ryan.

He turned on the TV to watch the day's news. He was shocked to learn they were still doing coverage of Chad Callahan, who had been murdered at one of the marinas—the guy who was with the IRA and had been hiding out for years. Evan wondered why some fugitives changed identities when on the lamb and others did not. Surely someone as smart as Ryan would have changed his name. Evan made a point to stop and see the local police and ask for their help if the photo prints turned out to be Ryan. He doubted the local police would be able to help him if a crime wasn't committed on Mallorca. Most likely they would advise him he'd be on his own if he wanted to make an arrest. No longer being an active cop, Evan knew he'd have trouble getting a warrant. He picked up his gear and left the hotel room in haste to see what the camera shop would be able to do for him, getting the film developed and blown up so he could see better details.

CHAPTER 23
Nick

Nick wondered just when Officer Lopez would come by to interview him. Although he knew he had nothing to hide except for the fingerprints on the bat, it still made him nervous to think about someone prying into his background. He parked his motorcycle, grabbed his helmet and headed to his boat. He could still see the yellow crime tape which was now around the back of Chad's boat, but the pier was open to traffic since residents and visitors needed to use the walkway to get to and from their boats.

Except for this gnawing frustration about getting interviewed, he felt he had a great day with Cassie. She was proud of his work and accomplishments, and he enjoyed working with her. It was almost like Nick, his persona, was real, and that he had started a new life. He couldn't undo his past nor overlook his mistakes with his employment at

Gaspard Yachting, or the murder of Armond, but he'd gotten himself in trouble by trying to accommodate clients who insisted on having high-quality cocaine on yacht rentals. He had a perfect setup arranged if it weren't for Armond snooping around and finding out he'd embezzled money from Gaspard to pay for the cocaine. The yacht rental business was highly successful and he'd made a lot of money for Gaspard. Had things not blown up, he'd always planned to put the embezzled money back into the company, but things got complicated and he instead put the money in off-shore accounts. Gaspard's biggest mistake was asking him to do the controller's work after he had murdered Armond. So convenient and an easy way to change the accounting spreadsheets. Lost in thoughts, he almost didn't hear the knock on his galley door. Reluctantly, he stood, took a deep breath and opened the door.

Officer Lopez stood at the door with the female officer who'd been at the scene of the crime. "This is officer Cortina. She'll keep notes while we talk."

Nick motioned for them to sit inside on the galley cushions on each side of the table. "Would you like anything to drink?" Nick asked, feeling stupid about asking, but he did have refreshments.

"No thanks, but appreciate your asking."

Nick sat on a cushion opposite both of them, resting his hands on the table. He could feel the tension in the air, and sat stoically staring at both of the officers. Officer Cortina was rather young, maybe thirty-ish, with her black hair pulled back into a bun at the nape of her neck. She smiled at him. "Nice boat. Have you had it very long?"

Nick swallowed. Knowing there would be a record of when he bought it on the island, he said, "No not that long."

"How many people does it sleep" Officer Cortina probed.

"Eight comfortably. There are three cabins, plus the main cabin, which I use because it's the largest."

"Have you been sailing much recently?" She looked around at the teak wood on the walls and ceiling.

Nick took a breath. "Not much time to sail since I started working."

"Oh, that's right." Officer Lopez commented. "You said you started a new job as a construction foreman, right?"

Nick forced a smile. "Yes, I work for *Cielo*, the new hotel under construction on the island."

"How long have you worked there?" Officer Cortina busied herself taking notes.

"Couple of weeks." Nick started chewing on the inside of his cheek to steady his nerves.

"So, tell us about your relationship with Chad Callahan," Lopez requested.

"Not much to tell, just as I told you this morning. We had been boat-mates. He was rather hard of hearing, left his television on late on a high volume. We bandied back and forth about the noise, mostly me asking him to turn the volume down so I could sleep at night."

"You asked him?" Officer Cortina tilted her head with pursed lips as if she didn't believe him.

"I started asking him, to no avail, so I often yelled to him so he could hear me."

"Did he turn down the volume?" Officer Lopez stared directly at him, making him unsettled.

"Look, the guy was old, deaf and boozed out many nights. We had words, but nothing that got ugly."

"That's not what Mrs. Delmonico said," Officer Cortina interjected.

Nick rolled his eyes. "I'm not surprised. She's a bit of a busy-body with an attitude. I probably was too loud on occasion. No doubt I upset her with our bantering."

Officer Lopez motioned for Officer Cortina to leave. Both got up, extended their hands and thanked Nick for his time. Nick stood on the deck of his boat waiting for them to leave before heading back into the galley. He was famished. Nerves on end made him ravenous. He poked around in the refrigerator, selected a half-eaten roast beef sandwich and sat down at his table. If ever he looked forward to going to work, this was it. For once in his life work was satisfying—no

92

murders, no embezzlement, no cocaine to proffer for wealthy clients—just a normal life working for a woman he liked and admired. Despite his unfortunate background, he believed he could go straight and not be on the lamb. He wondered where Evan and Danielle might be but decided it was not likely either one would be showing up at the *Cielo.*

Even if Evan were still a cop, which he wasn't, it's not likely he would come up to the *Cielo* and start looking for him. Nonetheless, he decided to work most of the next day in the trailer where he was not visible. Fortunately, the trailer was down the hill in the back of the hotel where no one could easily find it. He decided to take his chances and keep an eagle eye peeled just in case one or both showed up on the premises.

The hotel was nearly completed except for the furnishings. Carpet was installed and finishing touches were being made in the guest rooms, main lobby and spa. The pool needed to be pebble-tec'd, but other than landscaping, the project was on schedule. He had a good crew where everyone did their job and did it well. It was not likely anything would go wrong. He munched on his sandwich, opened a half-eaten bag of stale potato chips and settled in for the night with local television.

CHAPTER 24
Nick

Nick arrived at work the next day looking forward to logging in received materials and working with Cassie on details for the hotel's completion. He parked his motorcycle in the hotel's lot, set his helmet on the seat and headed up the grade to the hotel. A cool fog wafted in drifts as he walked to the hotel.

He was dismayed to see the crew huddled outside the hotel and not working. They separated when they saw him, revealing hideous black graffiti sprayed on the front of the hotel's entrance walls. Shaking his head in disgust, he talked to one of the workers who spoke fluent English and Catalan. "Do you think we can paint over this? Cassie has to be very upset."

Ricardo nodded. I've not seen her on the premises this morning. Since she works in the trailer, we knew not to bother

her unless it was an emergency. I knocked on the trailer door around 8:00 this morning, but she didn't answer. We'll have to order the stucco and reapply it, since the paint color was blended in the stucco. It will be expensive, but is the only way to cover the mess."

"Was there any other damage?" Nick asked.

"Nada." Ricardo responded.

"Do you know if it's kids messing around or a gang that's responsible for this?"

"Si. There are some paid gangs on the island—how you say, corruption and bribery. Lots of competition—some hotel owners don't want any more hotels on this island. Other's don't want more water restrictions—water is scare."

"That's disturbing," Nick said. "Let me see if I can locate Cassie and I'll get back to you. Go ahead and reorder the stucco to repair the damage. I'll see about any insurance claims and whether we need to put up a security camera on one of the entry columns."

Ricardo nodded affirmatively, spoke Catalan to the other workers who then disbursed and got back to work.

Nick walked up the hill around the side of the hotel and down to the trailer. As he reached for his keys, he noticed the opening to the trailer door's frame was bent and the door was slightly ajar, which he thought odd and worrisome. He climbed up the steps, entered the trailer and saw Cassie with her head sideways on her arm resting on the desk as if she were sleeping.

"Cassie?" he called out to her.

She didn't answer. It frightened him. He went around to the side of her desk and gently prodded her shoulder calling out her name. She didn't move.

He moved the chair, bumped into the desk and stumbled backward. "Oh my God! She'd been shot." Blood had dripped down her blouse to her slacks and on to the floor. Panic ensued and he immediately checked her neck for a pulse. Her skin was cold and clammy. Miraculously, she was still alive, but barely, and unconscious. Someone had shot her in the right side of her chest above her breast near her shoulder. He checked her back for an exit wound but there was none. He fumbled for his phone and dialed emergency. "Send an ambulance immediately—a woman's been shot in the chest, but she's still alive." His voice cracked and his hands shook. Sweat rolled down his forehead and the side of his face. He gave the location to the operator and set the phone down. He was afraid to move her for fear of making her injury worse. Running to the bathroom, he grabbed several hand towels, placed them under her blouse and pressed them gently against the wound. He then called the police and told them she'd been shot, gave them his name and said the ambulance had been called to take her to the nearest hospital. His army training kicked in. Fearful she was in shock, he gently picked her up, put her on the floor and elevated her feet. How long had she'd been like this? He covered her with his leather jacket.

Rattled, he flew out of the trailer, stumbled down the steps, caught his heel and fell to the ground. He got up, ran to the hotel yelling for Ricardo. With the construction noise, and hundreds of rooms he might be in, he wasn't able to locate him so he motioned to Benecio, one of the workers, to follow him. They both ran to the trailer, stumbling on the gravel as they headed down the path. "Stay with her," he indicated with his hands, not sure Benecio understood him, although he nodded. "I've called an ambulance," he said. "I need to be out front to show them where this trailer is located." Benecio nodded affirmatively. Nick sprinted out of the trailer, back up the hill and to the front entrance to the hotel where the ambulance would arrive. He frantically rubbed his forehead, his hands shaking with fear. Ricardo spotted him running. "Something wrong, Mr. Fontaine?"

"Cassie's been shot! She's still alive. One of the crew, Benecio, is with her. I've got to wait for the ambulance."

Ricardo's eyes widened with panic as he turned and ran toward the trailer.

How long it would take for an ambulance to drive up the long serpentine road to the hotel? Would Cassie still be alive?

CHAPTER 25
Evan

The camera shop was very accommodating. They would have the film developed and blown up for him so he could get a better look at the photos he took, which were too small to get a clear facial view on his camera. It would be a couple of days for the enlargement, so there was nothing to do but wait to see if the photos he captured would look anything like Ryan Coltrane. What do to do in the meantime? Although he wanted to go to the police and explain his predicament, he felt it would be far more professional to wait until he had evidence that Ryan Coltrane was still alive.

There was nothing left to do but tour the island. He promised himself that he would bring Danielle back to this place, show her the beauty she missed. Somehow, he'd make up for the emotional fight they had. She'd forgiven him, but he wanted to do something for her since they never had a chance to see the island together.

Because his love of architecture had been enhanced by years of study at Parson's School of Art and Design, Even decided to visit the Cathedral La Seu, deemed the most precious architectural treasure of the Balearic Islands. Wonderfully lit up at night, it is regarded as one of Mallorca's most photographed Gothic structure. He knew it was nearly destroyed by an earthquake in 1851, later repaired by Juan Bautista Peyronnet, and then one of his favorite architects, Antoni Gaudi, modernized the interior. He was excited to see the museum's precious works of art. Vowing not to miss the Museu de Mallorca, since it was very close to La Seu, with medieval and Baroque paintings—viewing fine art was always something he could pass the hours enjoying.

He recalled fondly when he first met Danielle they had agreed to meet at an art museum—he planned to teach her the difference between Impressionist and other modern artists such as Picasso. The Maeght Foundation in St. Paul-de-Vence, where they agreed to meet, was supposed to be the place they were going to tour together—he would be telling her the details of work by Chagall, Bonnard and Leger—but she didn't show up at the agreed upon time. He remembered being disappointed that she didn't arrive, only later to understand that her father's controller, Armond, at Gaspard Yachting had been murdered.

He thought it would be fun to tour Museu de Mallorca to understand the Mallorcan history and see the archaeologic excavations, Moorish ceramics and priceless medieval and Baroque paintings. Also, he wanted to see La Granja, a country house in a wooded valley near Esporles belonging once to the Fortuny family and built for King James II. These sites, in addition to the splendid beauty of the island, would make him a worthy tour guide. As he walked the streets near Valldemossa, with its wonderful restaurants, he marveled at the flora and fauna, the Crested Coots and the Sardinian Warbler with its distinctive cry. And there was the Stilt who loved the shallow waters and brackish ponds—an exceptionally noisy bird no one would want under their bedroom window.

He was impressed with the lush vegetation, the pomegranate, olive and pistachio trees, the carob and cypress. Of course, he loved St. Paul-de-Vence for its splendor atop a pinnacle—a spectacular city on a hill high above the Mediterranean with charming shops, art galleries, restaurants, ramparts and stone edifices and endless cobblestone streets. Mallorca had a breathtaking charm all its own: stone houses with surprising emerald green shutters, flowering window boxes with ivy and bougainvillea trailing up ancient stone walls. People were friendly, welcoming and hospitable. This, and other unexplored islands of Menorca and Ibiza were ones to be visited with Danielle on a future vacation, if she was willing to come back here for the honeymoon they didn't have.

Before going back to the hotel, he stopped by a café for a cappuccino and a blueberry scone, marveling at the weather, balmy at the beaches, but arid inland. Thoughts of her smooth skin on his, making love to her until he could hear her cries of passion matching his was something he missed desperately— all fleeting thoughts leaving him feeling bereft as he drank his coffee.

Thankfully, the hotel agreed to keep his room reservation open, so that if three weeks became four or five, they could accommodate him without moving him out of the hotel in busy tourist season. They said they couldn't promise him the same room, but would be able to give him a similar accommodation. Danielle had left some clothing behind. He'd put his head in the closet more than once to breathe in a scent that was familiar, as if she were still there. He felt responsible for ruining their belated honeymoon-vacation, but if he had been the one to spot Ryan instead of Danielle, it might have ended badly for both of them.

He wondered what Ryan might be doing at *Cielo*? It's not like yachting had anything to do with hotel management, but he did recall that Gaspard, Danielle's father, had given Ryan the controller's responsibilities—long before Gaspard found out that it was actually Ryan who killed Armond.

CHAPTER 26
Nick

Nick was relieved to hear the sound of the ambulance in the distance, no doubt winding up the treacherous road as quickly as possible. He stood helpless, full of anxiety, in front of the hotel's entry gates until he saw the ambulance arrive. "Hurry! She's in the trailer in the back. You'll need to carry a stretcher up this short hill and down the backside where the trailer is located."

The ambulance driver and two EMTs scurried up the hill with the stretcher, Nick following close behind, panic still running through his veins.

They entered the trailer bringing the stretcher with them through the trailer door. The EMT asked, "How long has she been like this?" Benecio stepped aside as the EMT knelt down to take her pulse.

"I don't know. I found her like this when I came to work at 8:00."

"She's lost a lot of blood. Let's get some fluids running through her." The EMTs carried Cassie up the embankment and down the hill and got her settled into the ambulance.

"Can I ride with you?" Nick asked, his voice pleading. "I'm her manager. She has no family here. I don't want her to be alone."

"Normally we don't allow it, but you can ride to the hospital."

Nick settled on a bench in the back of the ambulance watching EMT's place an oxygen mask on her face—a face so close to death, nearly devoid of color.

The ambulance roared down the Tramuntana, siren blaring in route to the hospital. Nick felt helpless watching while the EMTs attended to her, giving Cassie some sort of shot and hooking her up to an IV. What seemed like a panic-stricken long ride finally ended when they reached the hospital's emergency entrance. Attendants ran out of the hospital, took the gurney and rushed Cassie to surgery. Nick ran after the gurney with the doctors trying to give them information. "She's been shot," Nick hollered. "I found her this way when I arrived at work this morning—thought she was sleeping at her desk until I noticed all the blood."

"Are you next of kin?" The attending doctor asked.

"No. I work for her. I'm her construction manager."

"Wait here," the doctor said. "We'll let you know as soon as she's out of surgery."

Nick, feeling helpless, watched the gurney being pushed down the hallway. His head spinning—he'd left the crew back at the hotel without any information, except Benecio and Ricardo knew she'd been shot. Hopefully they'd explain that to the rest of the workers. He hadn't locked up the trailer and wondered with the bent door frame if it would be possible to do so. Whoever shot her must have known who she was. Most likely the police were on their way. No one would be at the trailer to help them gather evidence. He hoped Benecio would talk to Ricardo and explain what happened. Nick slumped down in the waiting room sofa. His fear escalated. He leaned forward, his face in his hands, elbows balanced on his knees. What if Cassie didn't make it? What would happen to the hotel? Should he notify anyone? He remembered she had mentioned talking to her father, but did not recall his name, nor did he have a phone number for him in Barcelona. Her cell phone was still on her desk. He hadn't thought to grab it. He'd take a taxi back to the trailer, check her phone for contacts. Maybe her father's name would come to him. He felt terrible about leaving the trailer unlocked.

He looked at his watch. Two hours had passed but it seemed like four. If she didn't make it, he'd be out of a job which was the least of his worries. He walked to a vending machine, selected a black coffee and went back to the waiting room.

Finally, he heard footsteps coming. "Doctor, is she going to live?"

"We'll know in the next twenty-four hours. She's very weak—in critical condition. We removed the bullet. It didn't puncture her lung and missed her shoulder blade. She's very lucky to have been shot on her right side instead of her left or the bullet could have entered her heart. We'll keep her in ICU until further notice. Leave your name and number at the admitting desk and we'll call you when we have more information."

Nick wandered aimlessly down the hospital hallway to admitting. "I'm Nick Fontaine. Cassandra Benoit was brought in a short time ago. I'm supposed to give you my phone number so you can call me when she's out of ICU. She doesn't have any family on the island."

"Do you know her date of birth? Insurance coverage?"

"No, I'm sorry. If she survives, I can ask her for that information."

"Can you call me a taxi? I need to get back to the trailer."

The desk attendant nodded and placed the call. Nick waited outside, numb with fear and noticed the taxi driver pulling up.

Nick sat in the taxi unable to carry on a cohesive conversation with the driver. He felt like he should talk to

Ricardo, if he was still there, so he could explain to the rest of the crew in a language they would understand. Seemed like they should stop working, however, he knew that would not be what Cassie would want. Several shipments were expected in the next few days and someone would have to be there to receive them or postpone the deliveries. He had numerous invoices to log in and needed to check the computer spreadsheets for discrepancies.

Oddly enough, his head wasn't pounding. He'd been too upset to worry the chemistry in his head. Most likely, he'd have a monster blinding headache later. The taxi driver dropped him at the front of the hotel where he spotted a police car. Several workers were sitting on the front steps talking. He thanked the driver and walked up to them. "Dónde esta' Ricardo?"

One of the crew got up and scampered inside the hotel, presumably looking for Ricardo.

Nick sprinted to the trailer and found yellow crime tape around the scene, one officer outside, and another officer inside.

"I'm Nick Fontaine, the construction manager here."

"Detective Brasco, and this is Sgt. Sandoval."

"Can you tell us what happened?" Detective Brasco said with his hand on his hip, just above his weapon.

Nick cleared his throat, knowing this was second crime he was witness to within a week. Chad had been murdered and now Cassie has been shot. He was beginning to feel as if he never left Gaspard Yachting and the crime he committed.

"I found her slumped over her desk this morning. I thought she was sleeping. I couldn't awaken her, touched her shoulder and the chair spun away from me—I noticed all the blood. It was obvious she'd been shot."

"Do you know of anyone who would want to hurt her?" Sgt. Sandoval asked, twisting his lips and making his grey-streaked moustache bend to one side.

"No. I'm not aware that she has any enemies. The crew is absolutely very fond of her—she's a tough task-master, but fair and considerate."

"Did you notice any damage? Anything missing?" Detective Brasco said.

Nick shook his head. "I didn't get a chance. I was so rattled when I saw that she'd been shot."

Detective Brasco rubbed his chin. "Is there a safe? Any money missing?"

Nick flinched. "Are you thinking this was a robbery? There's not a safe I know of. The crew is paid weekly from entries that Cassie, I mean Cassandra, pays on line through the bank. Deliveries are paid by invoices, and she writes checks from her business banking account. If she has any cash here, I'm not aware of it." Nick said.

"We're going to have to ask you to take a day or two off while we dust for fingerprints," Detective Brasco indicated.

"That's understandable. I'll tell Ricardo, who's pretty much is in charge of the workers. It's going to be upsetting for them to lose pay, but maybe they won't mind having a few days off."

"Where can we reach you?" Sgt. Sandoval asked.

Nick gave both officers his cell phone number.

"Where were you last night?" Sgt. Sandoval asked, his thin-lipped smile becoming intrusive.

"I live at the marina. I have a sailboat and I was on my boat after work and all night."

"Can anyone vouch for that?" Detective Brasco said.

Nick shrugged. "Doubtful. I don't mingle much with other boat owners."

"Come to think of it, you look familiar." Sgt. Sandoval said with a quizzical look on his face.

Nick felt his heart skip a beat like dead weight in his chest. "I think I was on television when that Irish guy, Chad Callahan, was murdered. I was standing near the crime scene talking to Officer's Lopez and Cortina."

"Hmm. Murder and attempted murder seem to be following you around."

Nick frowned and shook his head. "So, it would seem."

"I hate to leave the trailer unlocked. I can lock it up for tonight since it's getting dark, and be here first thing in the morning. Will that work for you."

"Well, it's not protocol, however a forensic specialist can't be here until tomorrow anyway."

"I will lock the trailer now. No one else has keys."

Detective Brasco asked, "Do you think the door will lock with its bent frame?"

"I don't know. Let's give it a try," Nick said.

Despite the askew door frame where the killer jimmied the lock, he hadn't damaged the deadbolt. Nick locked it and turned to both officers. "By the way, did you notice the graffiti on the front of the hotel?"

"We did see it. Vandals, I suppose. There's a lot of opposition to new hotels being constructed on this island, not to mention water rights."

Nick asked, "What about gangs?"

"We're looking into that as well. Often the graffiti will be signed by those claiming their territory. We'll see if the crew recognizes any of the symbols."

Nick said goodbye to both officers, then headed to the hotel to ensure the main doors of the hotel were locked. As if walking in a fog, he put one heavy foot in front of the other. He felt like he'd aged several years in the last five hours. He walked to his motorcycle but didn't notice a skunk before it was too late—the dammed skunk turned and sprayed his leg and the back wheels of his motorcycle. He pinched his nostrils in disgust, knowing he'd have to stop at the grocery store for some hydrogen peroxide and tomato juice. It had been one hellish day. He checked his phone for any messages, but nothing yet from the hospital. It would be a long wait for any news. What if she didn't survive the operation?

CHAPTER 27
Danielle

The first night Danielle spent alone without Evan was torture. Although the house he'd bought for her was everything she ever wanted, none of it meant anything to her without Evan.

She curled up in a blanket on the beige leather sofa in the living room, put on some music and tried to read a book, to no avail. Simon and Garfunkel's *Sound of Silence,* with the lyrics like *'hello darkness my old friend'* only pulled at her heartstrings making her feel more alone than she had in her entire lifetime.

Trevor was asleep in the bedroom. Having a child, their child, was so wonderful, so fulfilling. However, when Evan wasn't there, Trevor was a reminder of what her life would be like if she was a widow. Although her family, large as it was, was there for her, the idea of raising Trevor alone would be unbelievably painful. Trevor looked like Evan at eight months with his dark hair and impossibly captivating blue eyes—would be a daily reminder of the man she deeply loved if she lost Evan.

Sleep had been fitful. She felt exhausted. During the day, she was busy caring for Trevor, giving him a bath, feeding him his favorite foods, like pudding, and playing silly cuddly, laughing games. It passed the time because she wasn't thinking of Evan at those moments. Although when Trevor did something very funny, she wished Evan could've seen his antics. She vowed to keep her cell phone handy to capture these moments that might not come again. It was always enjoyable to watch him giggle, which made her laugh and warmed her heart.

Alexa's playlist moved from Simon and Garfunkel's *The Sound of Silence* to The Righteous Brothers, *You've Lost That Loving Feeling*. Tearing up, she barked at Alexa to play the motion picture soundtrack *Out of Africa*. This was one of her favorite movies. She adored Robert Redford and Meryl Streep, however in that movie it dawned on her that he died in the end—too upsetting. As soon as Trevor woke from his nap, she vowed to take him for a walk in the stroller because music was making her depressed. In two or three hours, Evan would call her and fill her in on what happened during the day, whether the photos showed enough of a picture to determine if the man she saw was Ryan Coltrane.

The sound of her cell ringing jolted her out of the doldrums. She recognized Chloe, her younger sister's number.

"Hey sis. What's going on?" Danielle asked.

"Nothing much. Just wanted to check in on you. I'm worried about you being alone."

"I've got Trevor to keep me company, but this house feels so empty without Evan. He bought me a large house and now I'm all alone in it."

Chloe offered, "Do you want me to come over? We could open a bottle of wine and chat—maybe watch a movie?"

"I'd love that. You always seem to know what I need. We could talk and then watch a movie.

"Sounds good. I'll be over in a half-hour or so. Okay?"

"Wonderful. See you then."

Danielle was grateful she could rely on Chloe whenever she was in a difficult situation.

The doorbell rang. Danielle jumped up to greet Chloe. "Hey sis."

Chloe hugged Danielle then smoothed her auburn tresses off her face. "It's going to be okay, you know. Try not to worry so much."

"Want some wine?" Danielle said.

"Sure. How about a wine spritzer?"

Danielle went to the kitchen and returned with two glasses of wine, some sliced cheese and crackers and placed them on the coffee table.

"Do you remember what my relationship with Evan was like in the beginning?" Danielle asked.

Chloe settled into the opposite end of the sofa. "What I recall most was how hard it was for Evan to think about having children. He didn't want them because if his deep-rooted guilt of not being able to protect his little sister. Ashley's death was such a horrific tragedy. It tore at his heart until he closed it from any idea of having children."

"Yeah, and the panic I felt learning I was pregnant and not wanting to tell Evan was a secret you and I shared—not even something I could confide to Mom. You were the one who convinced me to tell Evan I was pregnant and when I did, we had an awful fight. Evan was so shocked. How would I have known he had changed his mind about having kids. He was so upset I hadn't told him sooner. I was so relieved he wanted our baby." Danielle took a large swig of wine.

"But, don't forget, you didn't know you were pregnant for a while." Chloe said.

"Well, I had seen the torn condom on the carpet, but it was the only time we had sex. I was sure I wasn't pregnant. And then, I had a bleeding ovarian cyst to mimic my period? I felt shitty—dizzy, bloated, miserable. What an ordeal. Although I do recall the doctor telling me after surgery that my pregnancy would be just fine. I was shocked." Danielle grabbed a few crackers and slices of cheese. "I really appreciate your coming over to spend time with me. I miss Evan so much it hurts."

"Well, you are the one who left him in Mallorca. I don't intend to judge you, and I know why you left him there, but he has to feel very alone. It's not like Bob, his former boss, is helping him. He's on his own." Chloe said.

"I knew, if I stayed in Mallorca, we would just fight. I wouldn't want him chasing after Ryan—we don't even know if it is Ryan, but I'm pretty sure the guy I saw at the hotel was him. After all, I dated him—the guy who wanted to marry me, the daughter of the owner of the largest yachting charter company in the Mediterranean. He'd been dad's partner for over a year and there's no way I'd forget that face, or what he'd done. The few times we went out, I'd never have figured him for a murderer. Makes my blood run cold." Danielle looked into Chloe's eyes asking for understanding.

"We were all fooled by Ryan. He was a good-looking American. Here we were, inexperienced French women, enjoying his compliments and attention, although he never hit on me," Chloe said.

"You were lucky. I tried to be civil because he was dad's partner."

"Remember when Evan ended up in the hospital? "I was so glad I was on duty that night. Talk about trauma. Evan comes in nearly unconscious, bleeding profusely from his heel. That odious Morey eel bit him on the scuba diving trip with Ryan. Poor Evan panicked and tried to surface too quickly and got the bends. Thank God we have a hyperbaric chamber at the hospital. He was a mess."

"I can't forget that. You told me when he woke up after the operation that he thought you were me because we look so much alike." Danielle said.

"Yes, we do look alike, but I'm prettier." Chloe jested.
Danielle laughed. "I agree."
Chloe said, "I'm pretty tired. Can we skip the movie?"
Danielle smiled. "Sure."

"Do you mind if I take a look at sweet Trevor sleeping before I go?"

"Sure. I'll walk you to his room. There's a nightlight on."

"He's such a beautiful baby. Just think, I'm an aunt." Chloe whispered.

Danielle walked Chloe to the door, held her longer than a hug. "Thank you for coming. Although you are younger than I am, you are wise beyond your years. I'm proud of you. You're an excellent surgical nurse, grounded and committed to your profession. You've always had time for me, your older sister who seems to go from one crisis to another. Have I told you how much I love you?"

"You just did." Chloe smiled, turned and walked to her car.

CHAPTER 28
Evan

He'd had a nice conversation with Danielle last night but could hear in her voice how lonesome she'd become staying home alone with Trevor. His guilt continued to plague him. He promised her he'd try to get the stakeout film developed as soon as possible and was heading over to the photo shop this afternoon. This nightmare of her spotting someone who looked like Ryan had to come to an end. He wanted to be home with her, holding his son, Trevor, and going on with their lives.

He missed painting; several of his Jackson Pollock-like artworks and some of his landscapes were hanging in the Bogena art gallery in St.Paul, but he missed teaching art to the kids at Danielle's school. What a strange turn of events when his mother, Kelly, who graduated from Parson's School of Design, got him in to Parson's after he'd resigned from the El

Dorado police force following his sister's death. He never thought he'd be any good at art, and yet for a time it was an escape; then became a passion he thoroughly enjoyed. If he could just look at these damn photos and be sure one way or another if it was Ryan or not, he could get on with his life.

He entered the camera shop. "Hello. I'm Evan Wentworth. I have some enlarged photos to pick up," he said to the photoshop clerk. Evan sucked in a deep breath, nervous about what he would see. The clerk handed him the photos in a large brown envelope. He pulled out the photos—two were quite blurry, but the third and fourth photos, unmistakable—he'd captured the image of Ryan. "I'll be dammed!"

He stared at the blond hair, much lighter than when Ryan was working for Gaspard, but the countenance was undeniable. He'd also gotten a pretty good shot of Ryan's face from a front angle. What were the odds Ryan would be on this island? Evan tucked the photos back into the envelope, gritted his teeth, paid the clerk and hurried out of the shop to the car. He momentarily sat there, riddled with adrenalin, anger and determination to capture Ryan once and for all. Where the hell did he live? He was doing some work for the *Cielo*, work he couldn't imagine, but nonetheless, he was standing with a crew the day Danielle spotted him.

He called Danielle on his cell and waited in the car while the phone rang and went to voicemail. "It's me, hon. Call me as soon as possible. It's important. Love you."

The Palma police station was near the marina and took no more than twenty minutes to get there. Evan bolted out of the car, then turned and went back to the car concerned he wasn't thinking this through. His phone rang. "Danielle?"

"Evan, what's wrong?"

"You were right, hon. I had the photos taken at the stakeout enlarged. It's Ryan. I spent so much time with him on his dive boat, I'd recognize that asshole anywhere.

"I'm glad for you," her voice cracked, "but I'm really afraid. Now what?"

"I want you to mail me a pair of slacks and a dress shirt and my gun, with my Federal Firearms License, oh, and my work shoes. Before I go to the police station here, I need to look decent. I don't think there's much they can do, but I could use their help and will have more credibility if I don't look like a beach bum. The local police can tell me if I have any chance of extraditing him back to Nice."

"Okay, I'll do it. Are your gun and license in the garage? I can't remember where you keep them."

"They're in the locked cabinet above the workbench. The code is 4695. The gun isn't loaded, so don't worry about bullets. I'll get what I need here."

"You're scaring me, Evan. Do you have to do this?" Danielle pleaded.

"You know I do. I'll be careful. It's not like he's carrying a gun to work. Part of me wants to go up to the hotel, grab him and beat the shit out of him, but I will do this the right way or not at all."

"How's Trevor?" Evan asked, anxious to change the subject because he knew he upset Danielle.

"He's starting to talk and tries to say *m-i-l-k,* and *m-a-m-a,* making funny faces, but I can understand what he's saying. He makes me laugh."

"I wish I was there. I miss him so much. Once this is over, we will never have to have Ryan between us again," Evan said.

"I'll tell my dad about this because he's really worried."

"I think he'll understand. He knows how important this is to me."

"Call me tomorrow?" Danielle said.

"Absolutely. I love you, hon. I want this over as fast as possible. Do you have the address of the hotel?"

"I don't, but will look it up. You're still in our room, right?"

"Yeah. Send the package express mail."

"Will do. Evan?"

"What?"

"Be careful." Danielle's voice cracked.

114

Evan sighed deeply. "I promise."

He hung up the phone. The adrenalin subsided but he felt anxious. It was one thing to be wondering if the person Danielle saw was Ryan, but now to know it for sure frightened him. How he wished Ryan had died on the night he blew up his yacht. But no, instead he was a fugitive living and working in Mallorca.

If he and Danielle hadn't taken a belated honeymoon vacation to this island, chances are they'd never have known Ryan was still alive.

CHAPTER 29
Nick

Nick met the forensic specialist at the trailer at 8:00 a.m. along with Detective Brasco. The FS took a lot of fingerprints which Nick knew were his, but there wasn't anything he could do about it.

Detective Brasco said, "I think the person who shot Cassie wasn't very tall because of the entry angle of the wound in her chest. I noticed her cell phone was on the desk and her purse on the floor."

Nick nodded and grabbed both items. "I'll take these to her in the hospital. Will I be able to work here?" Nick wondered. "I have a lot to do without Cassie being here—deliveries are scheduled and I'm the only one besides her who is able to manage the accounting.

"Yes, you can work here. We'll send fingerprints to the lab, but other than that, we didn't find much. No footprints in the dirt we can use because there are so many. "You mind if I take your fingerprints? It will help us rule those out."

A chill ran down Nick's spine, but he nodded affirmatively. No sooner had he wiped the fingerprint stain off his thumb and fingers when his phone rang.

"Hello? Yes, this is Nick Fontaine."

Cassie's attending physician indicated that she was out of ICU. He could visit her briefly.

"I'll be there in a half hour or so," Nick said.

Detective Brasco waived a finger at Nick. "We'll want to talk to her too."

"Understood. Are you both done here? I want to lock up after we leave."

"Yes. We'll be in touch. Do you know where Cassie lives?"

"No, I'm sorry."

Both officers left the scene. Nick locked up the trailer and headed to the hospital.

He felt a tad silly walking into the hospital with a purse under his arm, but he knew Cassie would want to have it, along with her cell phone. "I'm Nick Fontaine," he said to the registration clerk. What room is Cassandra Benoit in?"

The clerk checked the computer. "She's in room 326. Elevator is down the hall on your right. When you get to the third floor, turn left past the nurse's station."

Nick nodded and headed to the elevator. Hospitals always bothered him—rooms of sick people, many who wouldn't get well, some elderly people waiting to die. He walked the long hall, aware of the light green wall paint and the sound of machines gurgling for patients needing oxygen. He found her room, peered in the doorway and noticed the first bed adjacent to the door was empty. Pushing past the curtain between the beds, he saw Cassie, her eyes closed with an oxygen tube in her nose to help her breathe. Some solution was being pumped intravenously. She looked so peaceful. Fragile. He hated to wake her.

"Cassie?" He pulled a chair up to sit next to her and lightly touched her arm.

She opened her eyes. "Nick. I'm so glad to see you." He reached for her hand without thinking and held it. She didn't resist. "How are you feeling?"

"Tired. Sore. Groggy," she said. "Could you open the blinds a bit more? I'd like to see outside."

Nick got up and adjusted the blinds. Sun streamed in across the bedsheet. "I'm so sorry this had to happen to you," Nick said, sat back down and reached for her hand again. "Do you remember anything?"

She shook her head. "Not much. I thought it was you coming into the trailer, because you have keys and no one else does. I was working on my credenza, so my back was to the door. It was locked, of course. I heard a grinding pop, I turned and someone dressed in black pointed a gun at me—it all happened so fast."

"Did you get a good look at him?"

Cassie shook her head. "No, he was wearing a gauzy mask of some kind."

"Did he say anything?"

"Go home. He said it in Spanish."

"Do you think he intended to kill you?"

"Maybe. But he could have shot me in the head and I wouldn't be here."

Nick took a deep breath. "Anything else you remember?"

"I reached for the phone. Apparently, I passed out. Did you find me?"

"Yes." He squeezed her hand tighter. "I thought you'd fallen asleep on your desk. When I tried to wake you, I pushed the chair aside and noticed all the blood. I knew you'd been shot. I went into panic mode. You had a very faint pulse, so I knew you were still alive."

She managed a weak smile. "So, you saved my life?"

He moved his fingers back and forth along her hand. "I'd like to think so.

I brought your purse and phone. The hospital needs to see your insurance card. Is there anyone you want me to call? You mentioned talking to your father, but I couldn't remember his name."

"Roberto. I'll call him later. He'll be very upset and will want to fly over from Barcelona to take care of me. I've been thinking I should move out of the trailer and into the hotel now that most rooms are finished. It will be a lot safer than working in the trailer. We could get an adjoining room," she teased.

"Best offer I've had today," Nick added and Cassie managed a light laugh.

"Anything I can get you? Magazines? A book?"

"You read?" Cassie quipped, the tone of her voice tinged with a smirk.

"Yes, I read," Nick laughed. "Nothing you'd probably enjoy unless you like biographies and history."

"I do. However, I also love romance novels, if that surprises you."

"It does."

Nick heard a knock on the door and a tall doctor with jet black hair entered. "Hello, Cassie. How are you feeling today?" His eyes radiated warmth and concern, peering at her just above his spectacles perched on the edge of his nose.

"Better, but I still have a lot of pain. I'm really groggy and tired."

"You're tired because we have you on a muscle relaxant and pain medications. You gave us a scare, you know."

Nick asked, "How long does she need to stay in the hospital?"

"I'd say at least three more days. She needs more rest than anything else," he smiled.

"Thank you, Doctor, uh?"

"Hardwick. I'm the attending physician. The ER team brought you back since you coded once, and we almost lost you." He pushed his glasses up to the bridge of his nose.

"Thank you for saving my life. When do you think I'll be able to return to work?"

"I'd say in two weeks. You're going to need physical therapy for your injury because your muscles and ligaments were damaged. We removed the bullet, which has been given to the ME for processing. Wounds heal from the inside out. We want to watch for an infection. For now, it's best you just rest. I'll check on you tomorrow. How's your appetite?

"Fair. I'd like some soup. My tongue feels furry."

Nick turned toward the door. "Speaking of soup, here comes the attendant with lunch."

Dr. Hardwick handed some papers to the nurse and left the room. A nurse asked how she was doing, checked her vitals then raised Cassie's bed up a few degrees and positioned her tray table over her bed, and then left the room. Nick moved aside and let go of Cassie's hand.

"Can you manage?" Nick raised his eyebrows.

"I'm right handed. Eating with my left hand is awkward. Maybe I can drink the soup."

"Or, I could feed you. I'm really good at balancing spoons."

Cassie laughed. "What's happening at work?"

"Not much. Because the hotel site became a crime scene, I had to let everyone go for a few days, but the police said I can work in the trailer. The door frame is bent, but the deadbolt works fine. I'll work there until you can return. Don't worry. I can handle the deliveries. I'll save the invoices for you to approve. By the way, the police asked if there was a safe in the trailer. They didn't find one, but considered a motive might be robbery."

"There's a petty cash box in my lower right desk drawer. I'll give you the key if you hand me my purse."

Nick took the key from Cassie. "I think I should be going. I don't want to tire you out any more than necessary. The hospital said I could visit you, but not to stay too long. Are you sure you're okay to drink that broth?"

She looked up into his brown eyes. "I'll be fine. Nick, thanks for everything you did. Without you, I wouldn't be here. It's a terrifying thing to know I'd been so close to death."

"You have a lot of years to live yet, Cassie." Without thinking, Nick got up and leaned forward to kiss Cassie on the forehead. It seemed like the natural thing to do—where boss and subordinate hierarchy no longer mattered. She caught his eyes smiling down on her and she smiled back as a woman, not his boss.

CHAPTER 30
Cassie

After Nick left, Cassie felt she no longer needed to put on a brave face. Her left hand shook as she drank her broth. As long as she was awake, she didn't have to fear closing her eyes. The sleeping pills gave her vivid, frightening dreams, but at least she wasn't lying in bed staring at the ceiling. She didn't feel rested, in fact felt exhausted. How could this have happened? Who would want her dead? The more she thought about it, she was rather sure whoever shot her didn't want to kill her, or they would have shot her in the heart or head. The assailant told her to go home, in Spanish, which meant he'd known she wasn't from Mallorca. Other than her crew, she didn't know anyone well on the island—some manufacturers, of course, had worked with her. She'd thought she had friendly relationships with vendors and suppliers. Was there someone she shouldn't have trusted?

Her worst fear was thinking the assailant would be back. She didn't feel safe being alone anymore, and certainly didn't want to think of going to her apartment and being alone. What if the killer did want her dead, was paid to kill her and just got off a bad shot? If his goal was to frighten her, he'd succeeded. What she needed to attend to was mind-boggling. She'd find a way to pay the crew for their days off, since they had families depending on steady income. Her chest hurt so much she couldn't imagine going to work, and yet she knew she needed to. Payroll needed to be processed for work the crew had already completed. She could teach Nick how to do it, but it would take time and he didn't know the Mallorca laws, standard deductions, and a whole host of paperwork that was difficult for someone who didn't manage payroll.

Then there was her father, Roberto, a wonderful man who was overly protective. She hadn't had the heart to call him because she knew how deeply upset he'd be. Mallorca was supposed to be a place where companies who added to the economy would be welcome—the tourist trade was the most critical to the island. How could one more hotel matter? The rooms in most hotels were booked solid for the key seasons. She had no idea who resented her or her hotel.

Thank God she had Nick to rely on—a good man who never questioned her authority, admired her work on hotel design and complimented her choices making her feel valuable. She loved architecture and design as much as running a hotel, and he seemed to share her love of construction. Building something from the ground up was like giving birth. Someone who didn't have a construction background would never understand the satisfaction one got from drafting something from an idea, to having blueprints made up, with an artist's rendering of the intended completed project. Watching the concrete being poured, walls being framed—the basic foundation of good design, and then seeing it come to life with all the details of beautiful design was thrilling. She wondered if she'd be able to manage her job responsibilities.

Her broth had cooled. Sipping it with her left hand was clumsy. Splatters ended up on the bedsheet. A wave of overwhelming fear consumed her. She felt tears welling up in her eyes and pool down her face. It wasn't like her to feel sorry for herself—quite the contrary. She'd excelled in architecture and drafting, as well as interior design, and had always been a determined, capable strong woman. Now, for the first time in her life, she felt vulnerable in a way she hated. She didn't have a gun, and never thought she'd need to use one. Going home in a few days and thinking about being alone in her apartment was terrifying. Did the assailant know where she lived? How would she protect herself and get the hotel projects completed? A knock on her door shook her out of her depressing thoughts. Two policemen entered her room and walked closer to her bed.

"Cassandra Benoit? I'm Detective Brasco and this is Sgt. Sandoval.

We're in charge of the investigation. Can we ask you a few questions? How are you feeling?" Detective Brasco asked then sat down in the same chair where Nick Fontaine had sat earlier.

"I'm doing okay—groggy and my chest is really sore, but I'm told I'm lucky that the bullet didn't lodge in any organs."

"What do you remember about the shooting?" Detective Brasco took out a small pad to take notes.

"It's hard to recall because it all happened so fast. I had my back to the door, heard a grinding sound—a pop, and thought it was my foreman, Nick, coming into the trailer. The noise startled me so I turned around, and this man said to me *veda casa*, in Spanish, to go home. Then, he shot me, turned around and left. It was split seconds. I wanted to call emergency, but apparently I passed out."

"Did you see his face?" Brasco said.

"No. His face was covered with a gauze-like black nylon stocking—very much like what you see in the movies."

"What height would you say he was?" Sgt. Sandoval inquired.

"I don't know, but he wasn't very tall—maybe 5'6" or so."

"What about the tone of his voice? Young, old? Anything you can tell us?" Brasco asked.

"His voice was hoarse—like someone who smoked a lot," Cassie replied.

"Anything else you can recall?"

She twisted her lips. "No. Sorry. I'm foggy about all of this."

Sgt. Sandoval asked, "Do you think he was there to rob you?"

"I doubt it. I don't keep much cash there. Why, was the trailer ransacked?"

"No, it was surprisingly clean. We think his intent was to frighten you. Unless he was a bad shot, if he wanted to kill you, you'd already be dead," Sgt. Sandoval said.

"I assumed as much," Cassie glanced up and rolled her eyes.

"Do you know of anyone who would want to hurt you?" Brasco asked.

"No! I'm really angry about that. I've worked with a lot of manufacturers and suppliers here on the island—everyone has been really helpful and nice to me.

Cassie's eyes started to pool, and she fought back tears not wanting to appear weak in front of the policemen.

Detective Brasco rose and pushed the chair back against the wall. "Thank you for your time. We'll let you know if we find out anything."

Both policemen turned and exited the room. Cassie felt frustrated and angry—angry to the point of wanting to get even with the person who shot her—the person who messed up her life, had taken her sense of security and accomplishment and flushed it down the toilet. How dare they?

CHAPTER 31
Nick

Three days went by in a hurry. Much to do at the office. Shipments of goods and materials coming in next week. Stucco repaired without a trace of the graffiti damage. He didn't have the heart to tell Cassie about the graffiti. She'd had enough distress with her bullet wound. Sgt. Sandoval had called and said the crew could come back to work. He recognized that with Cassie in the hospital, the hotel's completion deadline was at a halt. Putting all of the furniture in place in the hotel rooms required the crew to be back to help out, advising the movers where various pieces should go.

The window coverings company was sending installers in next week—so many details made his head spin: overwhelming details like which side did the cords for the blackout drapes go? Right? Left? He'd have to ask Cassie about that. Mirrors? How high were they to be hung? It was easier learning about construction details and an invoicing operating system for tracking expenses, but the design details left him feeling frazzled. This was a job for someone like Danielle's younger sister, Lena, the one who studied interior design. Unfortunately, he'd put her in the middle of the ocean, tied up to a dingy and nearly sacrificed her life, so that was out of the question—that and the fact that he was supposed to be dead. He wondered what Evan was up to? He hadn't seen him or Danielle. He'd half expected them to show up at *Cielo* looking for him, or worse, hauling him off in handcuffs as a fugitive. Maybe Evan and Danielle had left the island. He chewed on the end of a ballpoint pen, nervous energy with no place to expel it. The office phone rang and jolted him out of his worrisome thoughts.

"Hello? Oh, it's you, Cassie. I'm so glad to hear from you. How are you doing?"

Her voice cracked. "Struggling, I guess. I'm not okay."

"What's wrong?"

"I've had a terrible time sleeping, even with sleeping pills. I'll be somewhere in a dream and then I see him—the person who shot me, and it's like he's going to do it all over again. I wake up screaming. I screamed so loudly one night, the nurse had to give me a shot to calm down."

"Geez. I'm so sorry. When are you getting released?"

"This morning. I can't go home—I'm afraid whoever tried to kill me might know where I live. I'm terrified of being alone."

Nick could hear her crying over the phone. "Why don't you stay at my boat?"

"Could I? Do you have enough room? I don't want to impose," she sniffled.

"There's three staterooms. You can relax there." Nick felt his face flush at his own invitation, not thinking about her as his boss, just someone who had every reason to be frightened. "I meant to ask you. Your car must be at the hotel. Did you want me to pick it up? I'll come by the hospital, get your car keys, head back up to the hotel and get your car. I can leave my motorcycle at the hotel."

"I sure won't be driving for a while. I can't comb my own hair much less drive a car. It's like having my good hand tied to my back—can't do anything with it. Hurts to scratch my nose with my right hand and move my shoulder."

Nick chuckled, lightly, thinking of something to say to make her feel better.

"I'm good at scratching noses. Don't worry about anything. I'll help you get through this. I'll get your car. It will be easier to transport you."

Cassie sighed so loudly Nick could hear her breathing through the phone. "You still there?" Nick said.

"I'm here. I don't want to be a lot of trouble," Cassie said between sniffles. "Can you bring some of your clothes? A baggy shirt and shorts. Everything I had on is a bloody mess. I don't have anything to wear to leave the hospital."

"Sure. You're not any trouble. I'm glad to do it. I'll see you this afternoon."

Nick hung up and wondered if she would think it too improper to have her staying with him. However, she readily accepted his invitation. He shut down the computer system, set invoices aside, flipped on the new security cameras and floodlights he'd had installed both by the trailer and entrance gates to the hotel. They were set to go on automatically at dusk, but given it was late morning, he'd manually set the timers. He, too, wondered if the assailant would be back, not to mention whoever the person or persons were who did the graffiti damage. He hoped the floodlights and security cameras would be a sufficient deterrent. He knew, if the crime wasn't completed to the assailant's satisfaction, they would be back. Despite there being strict laws in Mallorca regarding gun possession, there was no way he was going to work in that trailer without his own gun which he got on the black market. He shuddered to think someone might break into the trailer and try to kill him. Seemed like he was fucked for trying to avoid violence, go straight, and lead a normal life. He gritted his teeth, slipped on his leather motorcycle jacket and headed out. Once again, he felt like a fugitive on the run.

128

CHAPTER 32
Evan

Evan unwrapped the special delivery package and took out his slacks, shoes, handcuffs and most importantly, his gun—a gun he hoped he wouldn't have to use.

To keep Danielle and Trevor safe at home, he kept his license to carry a firearm current. Never did he expect to find Ryan Coltrane alive, much less working on the island Danielle had chosen for a honeymoon vacation. He changed clothes and was pleased he looked more professional. He'd forgotten to ask Danielle to pack his gun belt, or he'd have nothing to strap his gun onto, but the smart woman he married packed it anyway. He was not planning on wearing his gun today, but had it in case he needed it in the future. He grabbed his enlarged photos he'd taken on the stakeout and headed to the Mallorca de Palma police station.

There were several police stations in Palma, so he chose one close to his hotel, halfway hoping he'd be going there again with Ryan in handcuffs.

He walked into the police station and greeted the desk clerk. "I'm Evan Wentworth, visiting here from St. Paul-de-Vence. Could I talk to one of the detectives here about a fugitive from Nice living here in Mallorca?"

"I'll see who's available. Have a seat. It will be a few minutes." The desk attendant left to walk down a long hallway. Evan sat down in the waiting room, leaned back in his chair and crossed his legs at the ankles. Wearing his shoes after being in flip flops for a couple of weeks felt odd. He was glad Danielle thought to pack a pair of socks. The police station was noisy, busy and crowded. He didn't expect there to be so much activity. He glanced around at the slate grey walls, odd shaped fluorescent dome lights in the ceiling, worn black leather chairs, two of them next to the one he was sitting in. A cigarette stand stood between the two chairs. Spartan surroundings. He pulled out his photographs and looked at them again—unmistakable photo of Ryan. He wondered what Ryan's name was now, assuming he changed his name. He'd obviously changed the way he looked with his longer hair bleached blond. Evan leaned forward and rubbed the back of his neck. He could feel his neck and back muscles tensing, dreading the conversation he would have. A door to the waiting room opened.

A tall, thin grey-haired officer approached him. "I'm Officer Santiago Lopez. And you are?"

Evan stood up and extended his hand. "Evan Wentworth. Retired detective from California, but I now live in St. Paul-de-Vence. Can we talk somewhere private?"

"Yeah, sure. Follow me to my office."

Evan followed Officer Lopez down a long hallway to his office, pulled up a chair and sat down. Officer Lopez sat behind his worn metal desk and clicked off his desktop computer screen.

"So, what can I do for you, Mr. Wentworth, is it?

Evan nodded. "This is going to sound absurd, but I can assure you every word I'm about to tell you is true. "Two weeks ago my wife and I were here on our honeymoon, well actually a belated honeymoon-vacation. We took a drive up the Tramuntana to the new hotel being built, *Cielo*, I think. She noticed a man who was working with a crew up there—a fugitive who escaped a murder wrap from Nice. He was declared dead, but obviously, he's still very much alive.

"Who'd he kill?" Office Lopez's eyes widened as he leaned forward.

"The controller of Gaspard Yachting in Nice."

"Ah, I've heard of that company. Very high-end yacht charters."

"Yes. The largest yachting company in Nice. My wife's father owns the company."

"How do you know he's supposed to be dead?"

Evan unfolded the photo he had taken at the stakeout. "This fugitive went by the name of Ryan Coltrane. After he killed the company controller, it took quite a while for me to think of him as a suspect, but my former boss, a local sheriff, in California came down to St. Paul. We were about to arrest him when he fled. The local police were heavily involved."

"You said he was dead, though?"

"Yes. He took a young woman, tied her to a dingy. It was one of Gaspard's daughters. He left Gaspard the coordinates on where to find her, and while we were working with the Coast Guard there, he had to be watching from some distance away. He blew up his yacht so we could see the explosion. The next day the Coast Guard and I checked the debris for a body, and we never found one. I always thought he staged his death, but couldn't prove it."

Officer Lopez's eyebrows knit together. "How did he get here?"

"Ryan was working with drug runners who supplied him with cocaine. The drugs were exchanged from a submarine to his boat. I assume someone picked him up and arranged for him to get to Mallorca.

"We're aware of these drug runners." Officer Lopez leaned forward.

Evan handed Officer Lopez the photograph. "This is the guy who's a fugitive. I did a stakeout adjacent to the *Cielo* hotel, and took these photos because I needed to be sure it was him.

Officer Lopez glanced briefly at the photo. His phone rang. "Yes, I'll be there shortly," he said. "Sorry, for the interruption. What do you need from us?"

"I know if I attempt to confront him, he'll run as soon as he sees me coming—most likely he has a gun and will try to kill me. Obviously, he doesn't want to go to prison or he wouldn't have faked his death."

"Well, unless he commits a crime here in Mallorca, there's not much we can do. We don't have an extradition treaty with France. Even if we did, extradition is a very complicated process."

"I was afraid of that. I thought of going up to the *Cielo* hotel and confronting him, but know damn well it would be a nightmare. I'm not looking to get shot. I assume he's working at the hotel, but don't know in what capacity."

"Doubt anyone's working there now." Officer Lopez said emphatically.

Evan frowned. "What? Why not?"

"Attempted murder. The manager, a young woman who was in charge of the hotel operation, was recently shot—survived, but it was a close call for her. The workers were let go until the preliminary investigation is completed."

"Do you know her name?" Evan said.

Officer Lopez typed in some information on his computer keyboard.

"Cassandra Benoit." Lopez said.

"I've heard that name before. My wife tried to call her to warn her—that's another long story, but was assured the person she saw was someone else—Rick or Dick, somebody, but that's all the name I have, and I'm sure it's an assumed name.

"Probably is. Did you close the case after he blew up his yacht?"

"Yes. Local Nice police had reported it in the paper."

"Why are you involved again?" Officer Lopez had a quizzical look on his face.

"Ryan Coltrane and his brother, Ted, were involved in a bank robbery in the states, in California. Several people were killed in the robbery, including my little sister, Ashley. She was in my squad car when bullets were fired. His brother, Ted, is the one who shot Ashley, but it's another long story as to how I found the connection between that robbery and the murder of the controller."

"I'm sorry about your sister." Office Lopez leaned back in his chair and put his hands behind his head.

"No more than I am—she was only six years old. I spent months trying to catch him, but by the time I was sure of what he'd done, he figured out we were on to him, so he faked his death."

"Do you mind if I make a copy of your photograph?" Lopez said.

"No, sure." Evan handed Lopez the photo of Ryan. The copy machine buzzed from Lopez's credenza. He handed the original photo back to Evan.

"Where are you staying?" Lopez asked.

"The *Calatrava*."

"Nice hotel. How long do you plan to be here?"

"Not sure. Until I resolve this case. I promised my wife I'd be home soon."

"Oh, she's not here? I thought you said you were on a honeymoon?"

"That's another long story."

Office Lopez shifted in his chair. "Fugitives make mistakes. Sometimes it takes years. They get too relaxed about their surroundings or interactions with people. Eventually someone recognizes them and ties them to their crimes. I hope that's the case with your fugitive."

Evan stood. "Well, thanks for your time. I knew it was a long shot. I want justice for my sister. She deserves it. The deceased controller, Armond, deserves it too.

"Understood. Be careful out there. If he's on to you, you'll be in danger."

"Don't I know it." Evan said, as he got up and left.

Officer Lopez opened another case he was working and set the folder on top of the photograph Evan had given him. Officer Cortina entered his office with a questioning look on her face. "Who was that guy?"

"Evan Wentworth, from St.Paul-de-Vence."

"What did he want with us?" she said.

"Complicated story. He's got a fugitive working here that he's trying to bring to justice, but he's no longer a cop."

"Good luck with that," she quipped.

"Yeah, that's what I told him."

CHAPTER 33
Nick and Cassie

Nick arrived at the hospital with a small duffle bag of clothing—sweatpants and a baggy shirt for Cassie. He had no idea what to do about underwear since he'd forgotten to ask, but would figure it out when he had a chance to talk with her. He approached her room and peered in the doorway. To his surprise, another patient was in the first bed now. He said hello and walked past the curtain to Cassie's bedside.

Cassie beamed a huge smile. "Thank God you're here. I'm so ready to get going."

"I brought you some of my 'get-out-of-the-hospital' clothes that should fit you."

"Appreciate it. We can stop at my apartment after we leave here—I need to pick up a few things—clean underwear for sure and some toiletries."

"Sure. Has the discharge nurse been here already?"

"Yes. As soon as I get out of this hospital gown, we're good to go."

She took the sweatpants and shirt and headed into the bathroom to change.

Nick smiled. "I'll wait for you in the hallway."

They left the hospital and drove to her apartment not discussing much besides the weather and hotel completion backlogged issues.

Cassie asked, "Do you want to come up? I'll just be a few minutes."

"I'll wait here, okay?" Nick sat in the car, engine running, nerves a little on edge. He had invited her to stay with him on his boat. Although inviting his boss to stay with him was rather unconventional, she'd readily accepted. He wanted to protect her. Having been shot in the shoulder during a bank robbery, he knew how much pain she'd endure while she recovered.

Cassandra returned to the car with a tote bag. "I'm ready to go."

They drove in silence with the car windows down. "Everything okay at your apartment?" Nick asked and glanced at Cassie.

"Yes, fine. I left the lights off so no one would think I was there. I enjoy having a ground floor apartment with a patio, but now being on the ground floor is the last thing I want. I closed the drapes. If someone is going to break in, they won't find me there." Despite the warmth of the sun on the car, she shivered in fear.

They arrived at the marina. Nick helped her out of the car, carried her tote bag and his small duffle bag to his boat. As they walked to his boat, they passed Mrs. Delmonico who was sitting on the deck of her boat. She pursed her lips and sneered at him, then gave a wide-eyed scowl of disapproval at Cassandra. Nick had never brought a woman to his boat, and in a small community of boat residents, this would probably be fast-spreading gossip. He had no idea why this woman disliked him so intensely, but assumed it was from his bantering with the now deceased Chad Callahan. All things considered, Nick knew he'd been sleeping much better without Chad's noisy television.

Nick helped Cassie on to his boat. "This is really beautiful, Nick. I had no idea you had such a gorgeous boat. How big is she?"

"Just under fifty-feet bow to stern," he said.

"Very impressive. I like the name of your boat, "*Slipped Away*.""

Nick smiled and helped her into the galley. "This is it. I'll show you to your cabin." He led her down a narrow hallway past the head, a small bathroom, to a cabin at the opposite end of the boat from his own quarters.

"This is beautiful wood. Is it teak?" She said.

"Yes. Lacquer gloss finish—holds up very well with the moisture."

She put her things down on the double bed, smiled at him and said, "I could use a drink."

"Wine, vodka, scotch? I have soda if you prefer."

"I'll take a vodka on the rocks. I'm not supposed to drink with the antibiotics, but one drink won't hurt."

"Are you sure?"

"I'm sure." She got up from the bed and followed him down the hallway. While he opened a liquor cabinet, she made herself comfortable in the dining area adjacent to the galley. "So, how long have you had this boat?"

"Got it shortly after I arrived here—less than year."

"Where'd you learn to sail?"

He hated to concoct lies, but decided half-truths were better. "In Southern California. When I was much younger, I had a job for the summer working for a boating company."

She smiled at him. "Do you take your boat out often? This island is one of many in the Balearic chain. You could sail to all of them."

"I've had her out several times and she's a dream on the water—handles very well, but her boom is cracked. Before I sail, I need to get the boom repaired because the horizontal side of the mainsail adheres to it. The mainsail is the larger one that captures the bulk of the wind. For a long time, I had some minnows clogged in the engine, and it stunk to high heaven, but had that repaired. Now there are other parts I need to order to get the engine running properly. If the wind is not there or quits when you are out sailing, you need a good engine."

She laughed. "So, we're marooned here?"

"Yes, my captive boss," he laughed. "We're marooned on a dock." He brought her drink to her and set it on the table. "Here you go."

She looked up at the décor, something she did automatically being an architect and designer. "Love the royal blue and white accents on the window coverings and furniture cushions. Oh, and I see your books stacked up on the book rack." She took a sip from her drink. "What did you read last?"

"*Unbroken*, by Lauren Hillenbrand."

"Good book?" she asked.

"Excellent WWII true story of Louie Zamperini's survival in a Japanese prison camp."

He sat down opposite her and swirled his drink around his ice cubes with his index finger. "Do you want anything to eat? I thought I'd ordered in tonight so you can just rest. Pizza? Chinese? Chicken?"

Cassie's face lit up. "I'd love a pizza because I can eat it with my left hand. Eating with a fork in my right hand is painful and trying to eat with my left is ridiculously difficult. Who'd have thought eating would be so hard from a gunshot wound?"

"It takes time," he said. "You'll be good as new with some physical therapy."

"Speaking of time, I'd like to lie down for a nap. I'm exhausted."

"Go right ahead. I'll run up to the hotel, check on things, see if mail has been delivered. If there are any invoices, I'll bring them back with me for you to review."

"You're the best. Thanks so much, and thanks for the drink. It's made me a bit tipsy."

He watched her get up and head to her cabin. Even in his sweatpants, she looked attractive. It was obvious she'd lost weight, but still, she was a beautiful woman.

The boat rocked lazily in the breeze. He opened two portholes to give the galley some fresh sea air. The very idea of her being here, and sleeping on his boat made him fully aware of her as a woman, not his boss. What was he thinking when he invited her to stay on his boat?

CHAPTER 34
Nick and Cassie

While Cassie was napping, Nick took a taxi up to the hotel to retrieve any invoices needing approval, and also get his motorcycle. Cassie could go to physical therapy with her car and he could go to work on his cycle. Her shoulder and chest ligaments were painful, but felt she could manage driving.

He stopped and picked up a pizza and two small salads for dinner. Oddly enough, he was happy to be taking care of her—not something he had done with anyone in the past. Gillian, a Columbian hottie in Nice, was the last woman he dated. She was fun, but heavily linked to cocaine trafficking and supplying him with the cocaine he needed for the high-end yachting charters when customers demanded it. He thought of the steamy nights they spent at her place and on his yacht, but he never felt like she was someone he wanted in his life beyond a fling.

Now, with Cassie on his boat, he felt differently about her than he had with any other woman. Cassie was a class act—intelligent, accomplished and very attractive. In another situation, where he wasn't her employee, he'd definitely be interested in dating her—and now, as a respite from being shot, here she was on his boat. He vowed to be on his best behavior and not hit on her because he didn't want to ruin their professional relationship.

Nick hauled the hot pizza and salads on to his boat and opened the galley door. "Hey, you're up. How are you feeling?"

Cassie covered her mouth with a yawn. "I slept like a dead person. Stress makes one very exhausted. When I awoke, I didn't know where I was. Something about being on the sea—the salty breeze, the lulling of the boat floating in the water—very relaxing. I smell pizza!"

Nick handed her a plate with a large slice of pizza. "You hungry?"

"Starved," she said reaching for the plate. "Thanks for the salad, too. That was very thoughtful of you."

They ate without talking watching gulls squawk and swoop around boats in the harbor looking for fish and food scraps. He poured her a glass of merlot and one for himself.

"So, tell me about yourself," he asked. "I really don't know anything about your background. Where did you grow up?"

"I'm an only child. I grew up in Besailu in the Girona region outside of Barcelona. Art and architecture fascinated me as a child. I used to watch my father sketch designs and pour over drafts that turned into blueprints. I think, from the time I was little, I wanted to be like him, so I studied architecture and design in college."

"What about your mom?"

"My parents divorced when I was twelve—a really difficult time for me, but I wasn't close to my mother. I think she resented me because I spent so much time with my father."

"You mentioned your mom. Is she still living?"

"No. She died of a brain aneurism—very sudden. I was at school. I remember a knock on the classroom door and the headmaster asked me to step outside in the hallway. My father was there. He knelt down and told me Mama had died. I went numb. For a long time, I felt odd to have only one parent. I missed her more after she was gone than I did when she was around, which wasn't often."

"Was she a stay-at-home mom?" Nick asked.

"No. She ran a small bakery shop in the village. Apparently, she keeled over one day at the shop, and just like that, she was gone. It took me years to come to grips with her death. Because she had died when I was young, I had to learn how to cook or my father would have starved. We're very close now. We rely on one another for support—it's just the two of us, and I'm okay with that. What about you?"

Nick didn't have time to craft a background story, so he made one up between bites of pizza and wine. "I, too, came from a home where it was just me, my brother and father. My mother left when I was a kid. My father was a very abusive alcoholic. My brother and I survived a lot on our own."

"I thought your dad ran a construction company?" she said.

Nick looked away from Cassie, as if caught in his own lies, when this was one person he wanted to be truthful with, but couldn't do it. "He did have a construction company. His drinking got in the way. It's not like he would get obliterated with alcohol on the job, but once he was home, it would take only one drink for his personality to change completely—he would get out of control, very aggressive, mean, obstinate and full of rage. When he died, I sold the company."

Cassie sighed and took a sip of her Merlot. "It's amazing to me how resilient children are given the challenges they have to put up with during their youth.

"I noticed the scar on your leg. How did you get it?"

Nick flinched. "Oh, that. Tour in Iraq. Shrapnel."

They sat and talked about the news, the weather, books, travel, and Nick did his best to relax. He felt like someone had plunged a knife into his chest. It hurt so much to lie to her— the one person in his life where he wanted transparency, and he couldn't reveal his true self. "Want to sit outside and watch the sunset?" He asked, hoping to break up the tension he felt.

"Sure. I'd like that very much. Before we go, I need to take these pain pills."

He noticed she had changed from his sweatpants to her own shorts and blouse. Her curves were obvious under her blouse and he couldn't help staring at her full breasts and her long, slim thighs and shapely calves. He did his best not to stare at her, and guided her to the deck.

The sun was a blazing ball of red and gold, sinking into the horizon rapidly.

Nick finished his wine, poured himself another glass and refilled Cassie's.

"What do you like best about sailing?" she asked.

"Everything. When the wind is just right and the sails are wing-and-wing, it makes you feel like you can accomplish anything—it's so freeing. All your fears are gone. Just the wind in your hair, the swell of the waves, the dipping of the bow or the tilt of the boat when you're turning—I find it the most peaceful place to be."

She smiled and caught his gaze. "When I've recovered, will you take me?"

"I'd love to," he said, and meant it.

They talked for another hour. He watched her shiver holding her arms. "It's getting chilly out here. Want to go in?"

She nodded. "Good idea. I don't want to catch a cold."

Nick said, "Why don't you watch TV while I swab the deck?"

She wrinkled her nose. "Need any help?"

"From a one-armed swabber? I don't think so," he laughed. "That's all I need is you falling down in the suds."

"Okay. I'll watch TV. Where's the remote?"

He pointed to the wall. "On the shelf behind the bench."

He cleaned the deck, rinsed it, and worked off tension. If she weren't so damn attractive, he'd be less nervous. It wasn't something he expected. After all, he'd been working with her side by side and never felt unsettled. Because she was on his turf, everything changed.

143

CHAPTER 35
Nick and Cassie

Nick cleaned up the dishes and set the leftover pizza wrapped in tin foil in the refrigerator. With the portholes open, music streamed in from another skiff.

A gentle wind rocked the boat from side to side. Nick and Cassie watched news on TV until they both became drowsy. Cassie had curled up on the cabin sofa bench with her feet tucked under a blanket.

"I think I'm ready to hit the hay," Nick said. "How about you?"

She blinked and rubbed her eyes. "Sounds good. I really appreciate your putting yourself out like this."

"Honestly, it's no trouble. You're an easy guest. The last thing I would want is you being alone and afraid in your apartment."

She nodded, tossing the blanket aside. "I'll see you in the morning before you go to work."

Nick stood and found himself in the same space as Cassie. They laughed and sidestepped one another awkwardly while his hand brushed her thigh and her hand brushed his arm. She wiggled past him. He watched her walk down the hallway, her long hair trailing down her back, her beautiful legs carrying her to her cabin.

He offered, "If there is anything you need, let me know."

"The pain pills helped a lot. I think I'll be fine," she said and waved to him as she turned and went into her cabin.

He shut off the lights and turned on a small amber fixture above the sink in case she got up during the night.

Nick tossed his T-shirt on the bed, pulled off his shorts and crawled under his duvet. With his hands behind his head, he stared at the ceiling wondering whether he would be able to sleep with a beautiful woman just down the hallway.

He realized he had dozed off when he heard muffled sounds that turned into a scream. He bolted out of bed rushing down the hall to Cassie's cabin. He could hear her screaming "No, no, don't, please..."

He knocked on her cabin door. "Are you okay?" He could hear her moaning and sobbing. He opened the door. She was sitting on top of the bed with her legs crossed, trembling. He went to her and sat on the edge of the bed.

"Nick, I'm sorry I woke you. I have these terrible nightmares—it's like the killer is coming, aiming that gun at me, and I can't stop him," she sobbed.

Her whole body was shaking. He leaned toward her and took her in his arms.

"You're having flashbacks from post-traumatic stress."

She put her arms around him, her head resting on his shoulder. Tears streamed down her face." He held her lightly. "Go ahead and cry. It'll relax you and make you feel better," he said.

They sat like that for a while. He let her cry as much as she needed to.

"Do you have some Kleenex?" she asked.

145

"No, but I'll get you some toilet tissue."

He returned to her cabin with a wad of tissue and a bottle of water.

She said, "The pain meds help with the injury, but they give me frightening dreams. I'm not going to take them anymore."

He stroked her hair and touched her shoulder. "You going to be okay, now?

I should go."

She met his gaze. "No, I'm not okay. Please stay." She shifted over on the bed and patted the space next to her.

A cool breeze wafted through the porthole. She moved down on the bed. Her breasts were firm and visible through her thin nightshirt in the moonlight. Her slim thighs and legs were nestled in the covers. He swallowed, not thinking of what was right or wrong, just what he wanted to do—what she wanted him to do. He shifted on the bed and laid down next to her, his heart beating wildly. She reached for his neck and pulled him closer.

He said, "Are you sure?"

She answered, "I've never been more certain of anything," and kissed him.

Her full lips awakened the pulsing between his thighs. The kiss was soft at first, then became intense and passionate. He wanted to make love to her, to become fully immersed in her scent and beauty, but with her injury, he was very tentative. "I want you," he said, "but I don't want to hurt you."

"You won't hurt me." She placed one leg over his and put her index finger on his lips and whispered, "Don't talk."

She removed the covers and kissed him with a hunger he had not felt in a long time. He removed his briefs and laid there, ready for her. She mounted him, sitting gently. They moved easily with her on top, his hand reaching for her breast, careful not to push into her shoulder. She moved in a circular motion atop him until he could no longer control himself. As she began to climax, he did too, holding her buttocks to him. Her cries of passion were intense. Afterwards, she moved off of him, exhausted but content. She nestled into him, her head resting gently on his shoulder.

He pulled the covers over them and put his arm around the back of her neck and sighed deeply, still tingling with warmth.

Her face in the moonlight was exquisite—her long dark eyelashes, the contour of her cheeks, the slope of her small nose. He closed his eyes, still in a befuddled state of bliss about what just happened, and knew nothing would ever be the same.

CHAPTER 36
Nick and Cassie

When Nick awoke, it took a few seconds for him to realize he was in bed with Cassie. Her eyes were still closed. Tendrils of dark hair had tumbled across her forehead. He looked at her sleeping so soundly with barely a breath escaping from her slightly parted lips—lips that held so much promise last night led to intimacy he couldn't have imagined. He turned on his side, propped up on his elbow and watched her sleeping peacefully—no nightmares after their coupling. He was completely exhausted, but in a good way. A smile crept across his face. What would he say to her once she woke up? He didn't have any recriminations, but wondered if she did, and would it be terribly awkward to work with her, or just easy? She stirred and opened her eyes.

"Morning," he said and stroked the tendrils off her forehead.

She leaned into him. "Morning already? I could sleep for several hours. For the first time since the shooting, I wasn't afraid. Thank you for staying last night. I didn't want to sleep alone. I never expected us to end up having sex, but I'm glad we did."

"So am I. You are a very beautiful woman. I thought you were stunning the first time I saw you, hardhat and all."

"Oh, that's right. I was working with the crew and you showed up looking for a job."

"Best decision I ever made," he smiled broadly, his fingers stroking the side of her face.

"I don't want you to feel awkward about our having sex and working together. I wanted you, needed you, and you were there, willing to share yourself with me. It calmed me down so I could relax and feel safe."

He leaned in to kiss her. She responded with a warm, affectionate kiss pulling him toward her. Her soft lips began to excite him again, but he didn't want to ruin anything by assuming she was someone other than his boss recovering from a terrible shooting. She was still very fragile—a fragility he knew as a child when he couldn't make the nightmares go away nor escape from his father's beatings.

He swung his legs over the side of the bed, pulled on his shorts and turned toward her. "You like eggs and toast?"

"Sure," she said. "You not only read good books, you cook too?"

"Nothing fancy, but when you live alone, you learn how to survive."

She yawned and stretched her arms. "I'd like to freshen up before we eat."

"Go ahead. There's plenty of hot water in the shower."

"Coffee? I'm useless without it." She rolled her eyes.

He did a thumbs up. "I'll make a fresh pot. Extra towels are in the cabinet below the sink."

She rose from the bed, grabbed her shorts and blouse and headed into the bathroom. The doctor told her not to get the bandage wet, so she was careful to only sponge bath the sweaty sex away from last night. After a refreshing partial shower, she dried herself off one-handed as best as she could, dressed and looked at herself in the partly steamed up mirror. She smiled at her reflection, her rosy cheeks, her contented expression on her face. If she didn't watch herself, she could fall in love with him.

CHAPTER 37
Evan

The waves broke close to shore as Evan swam under them further and further out to sea. His mind wandered between frustration and guilt about being on Mallorca for several weeks without Danielle. He had no idea where Ryan lived. He'd combed beaches looking for him, checked out coffee shops and local restaurants without any success. The idea of justice at all cost wore thin. Thoughts of Danielle living alone with Trevor gnawed at him, filling him with guilt. He tried to imagine what his life would feel like if he didn't pursue justice for Ashley. Armond Fouquet, a valued employee as Controller of Gaspard Yachting, his wife's father's company, died at the hands of Ryan Coltrane. There was no justice for either Armond or Ashley. He pondered the question: could he live with himself if there was no justice for either of them? He hated to admit it, but living like this on Mallorca alone without

Danielle, who should have been here to celebrate a much-needed belated honeymoon, was a too much of a sacrifice. He decided to call her and let her know he was coming home. Her cell phone rang three times and then she picked up.

"Danielle. How are you doing? I've missed you and Trevor so much it hurts. I've given this a lot of thought. There's no way I can work with the Mallorca police or the police I worked with in Nice to bring justice for Armond and it's impossible to link Ryan to the bank robbery in El Dorado Hills because that case is closed. I want to come home."

"Are you sure? What about justice for Ashley? I thought you couldn't live with yourself if you didn't punish the person who was responsible for her death."

"It's a sacrifice I'm willing to make. I've hated being here without you."

"I know. I've never felt more alone in my life," she said with a deep sigh.

"I'll look into booking a flight tomorrow. As much as I've tried, I haven't seen Ryan anywhere on the island, don't know where he lives, haven't seen him in restaurants or cafes. Due to the shooting at the *Cielo*, the hotel's construction had been halted, so Ryan hasn't been working up there either. It could be years living here before we'd run into each other. I don't want to sacrifice our marriage over this relentless pursuit of a criminal who can't be found, and even if I found him, there's nothing I can do with him. I can't arrest him, nor prosecute him," Evan said.

"Understood. I still feel it was my fault for spotting him in the first place."

"Not your fault. You couldn't help what you saw, and as it turned out, you were right. It *is* Ryan."

"Let me know when your flight is coming in and I'll pick you up from the airport."

"Love you, Danielle. Hug Trevor for me. Can't wait to see you both."

"Love you more, hon. I'm so happy you are coming home."

The call ended and Evan sat on the bed in the hotel suite relieved that he'd made a firm decision to end his search.

Despite deciding to relinquish his angst and dogged determination to find Ryan, he felt drained from a dull feeling of failure. His cell phone rang again. He thought it might be Danielle calling back. "Hello?"

"Is this Evan Wentworth?"

"Yes."

"This is Officer Cortina. You were at the police station a couple of days ago and met with Officer Lopez."

"Yes, that's right. What's this about?"

"I noticed the photograph you left with Officer Lopez. He told me where you were staying and gave me your phone number. Is this the man you are looking for?"

"Yes, why?"

There was a murder at one of our marinas a few weeks ago. We interviewed marina residents. I recognized his face when I saw your photo."

"Do you know where he is?"

"I not only know where he lives, I know his name. He goes by Nick Fontaine now. He lives on his boat, *Slipped Away* in the marina closest to your hotel. You're at the *Calatrava*, right?"

"Yes." Evan ran his hand through his hair. "Was Nick involved with the murder?"

"Unfortunately, no. It's a complicated story involving the IRA. A bombing that took place in Northern Ireland a long time ago."

"Oh! I remember hearing something about this guy on TV—Chad someone?"

"Yes, Chad Callahan. His boat was next to Nick Fontaine's."

"Thank you so much for this information. You have no idea what this means to me."

"I wish we could be of more help, but he hasn't committed any crime on Mallorca, so we can't arrest him."

"I understand. I know I can't arrest him either, but at least I can confront him about the murder he did commit."

"Understood. Don't get yourself killed," Officer Cortina said.

Evan hung up the phone and sat on the bed. Chills traveled down his spine.

He got up, grabbed his gun and a clip he'd purchased, put on his running shoes and left his room. His heart raced as he hurried to the elevator. He knew how dangerous this would be, but it was something he had to do.

CHAPTER 38
Evan

Evan ran to his car in the hotel parking lot with his nerves on edge. He sat in the driver's seat, fumbled with his keys, started the engine and drove out of the hotel grounds with a vengeance. The marina was close by. He wondered which boat was Ryan's. He wiped sweat from his brow. Anxiety overwhelmed him because he wasn't planning to kill Ryan, but he wasn't going to let him go on living life with no restitution for what he'd done either. He hadn't fought anyone in a long time, but the adrenaline rush pulsing through his body made him feel like he deserved to beat the crap out of Ryan, now living as Nick.

Gravel spit sideways on the road as his tires rounded turns. The sun was setting, a golden glow above the horizon, surrounded by rolling dark clouds. Possibly a storm coming. The air hung heavy with humidity. His t-shirt was already damp. He parked the car at the edge of the marina not knowing exactly what direction to go first to find the boat. Anxious thoughts ran through his mind—guilt that he hadn't booked a flight home yet, and if he told Danielle about the phone call from Officer Cortina, she'd be terrified. He fingered his gun as he got out of the car—a gun not to kill someone, but to protect himself if Ryan tried to kill him first.

He walked the dock slowly, looking at the names on the back of various boats, some smaller yachts, but mostly sailboats of varying sizes. The dock creaked under his weight while he looked to his right and left glancing at each boat. The sun glare made it difficult to see the names on the back of the boats. His breath came in short spurts. He willed himself to remain calm, but he was ready for a fight. Then, he spotted Nick standing on a boat embracing a girl in his arms.

He shouted out. "Nick Fontaine, I'm coming for you!"

Nick pushed Cassie aside almost knocking her overboard, dashed off the boat, jumped on to the dock and began running. Evan ran after him, nearly shoving people walking on the dock into the water. Nick ran to his motorcycle, got on and peeled out of the lot before Evan could reach him. He ran back to his car determined to follow Nick. Where was Nick headed? It was already getting dark.

Evan turned on his headlights and saw the motorcycle heading up through town. He backed out of the parking lot, rear-ended a dumpster, and sped after Nick who was weaving in and out of traffic. Evan hit his horn to pass cars whose drivers rudely responded with an arm flip in disgust. All of this would have been so much easier if he was still a cop, a cop with his own car and a siren, but that was all in the past.

He gained some advantage on the motorcycle and could see Nick was only three cars ahead of him, but Nick was passing cars on the right and left. Traffic was coming in the opposite direction and Evan had to be careful or he'd be dead before he could even get to Nick. That was it—"*vengeance is mine, sayeth the Lord,*" but this personal vengeance was a long-time coming. Evan followed as closely as he could. Where was Nick going? Oh shit, he's heading up the Tramuntana. No time to put on his seatbelt. Evan floored the gas and sped after Nick.

CHAPTER 39
Cassie

Cassie stood on the deck of Nick's boat wondering who the man was that was yelling at Nick and chased him down the dock. What did he want with him? Nick had been holding her and then suddenly he pushed her aside, so much so that she landed awkwardly on the bench cushions. Chills traveled up her spine despite the muggy hot air. Whatever the problem was between Nick and this other guy, there wasn't anything she could do about it.

From a distance she could see that Nick got on his motorcycle, which they had discussed earlier. He was going to *Cielo* and pick up the mail. Nick had taken his gun with him, and for that, she was glad. At least Nick had protection if someone was planning on doing him harm. Her hands started shaking. The more she thought about it, she wondered if the man chasing Nick might be the killer. What if the plot to kill her was only part of someone's plan?

Dark clouds moved across the sky with distant thunder. Raindrops began to fall lightly so she ran inside, closed the cabin door tightly and then locked it. The rain turned into a torrential downpour. Fear and a sense of helplessness surrounded her making her breathing shallow. If the killer was intent on further harm, he now knew where they lived.

She grabbed a towel from the bathroom, dried her hair, hung the damp towel around her shoulders and pulled it close to her. What could she do? Nothing. Absolutely nothing. She couldn't manage the drive up to the hotel—too much stress to her shoulder. If she called the police, what would she say? Some man came running down the dock calling Nick's name and Nick took off on his motorcycle? Hardly a scenario supporting police intervention. She thought it best to calm down and wait for Nick to return. Once he was back, she'd confront him for an explanation.

The rain was now pounding the boat, making it sound like she was living inside a tin can. She tried the television, but the reception was crackly and intermittent so she shut it off. Up on a shelf by the television was a rack of books.

Nick had mentioned he enjoyed *Unbroken*. On her tiptoes she reached for the novel with her good arm extending her fingers out enough to grab the book. It toppled off the shelf on to the floor. When she bent over to pick up the book, a photo fell out of it. She looked at the faded photo obviously taken some years ago and recognized Nick but did not recognize the other man. Handwriting at the bottom of the photo indicated Ted and Jed Reddiger. She stared closely at the photo. One image was definitely Nick Fontaine with a different name, but who in the world were Ted and Jed Reddiger? A wave of mild nausea overcame her and she steadied herself against the dining table. Was it possible that Nick was too good to be true? What if he wasn't Nick Fontaine? Who had she just slept with? Tears formed in her eyes. She sat on the sofa bench and pulled a blanket over her legs. There had to be an explanation. Nick had been an excellent employee. He'd filled in as her foreman with little training. The crew respected him. If anything, he'd saved her life and had been very protective of her.

She started imagining all sorts of awful possibilities. If he had another name, did he escape from prison? What had he done? She shivered feeling that vulnerability again she despised. Nothing made sense.

Nick's laptop was on the counter. She bit her lip and walked over to the closed laptop and stared at it. When he applied for the job, she hadn't asked for his resumè, but her father, Roberto, had checked the internet for her. Everything Nick told her about his past coincided with her father's internet search. She scratched around the bandage over her wound. It itched. She flipped open his laptop, stared at the password protected screen and decided she couldn't snoop even though she wanted to. It didn't seem right to snoop given the caring behavior Nick had shown her over the past weeks.

She vowed to ask Nick about Jed and Ted Reddiger when he got back. For now, all she wanted was a stiff drink. She poured herself a small glass of vodka and settled back into the sofa. Thunder and flashes of lightning had subsided. Steady rain pelted the sailboat. Thumbing through the novel, she started reading from page one. With the lousy weather, it could be a very long night before Nick returned. In a short time, she was completely engrossed in the book.

CHAPTER 40
Evan

Evan followed Nick up the highway as closely as he could. His Renault rental car was no match for Nick's motorcycle. The rain made it difficult to see clearly, even with his windshield wipers swishing on high. Nick was several cars ahead of him, but the motorcycle's tail light was bright enough that Evan could see him. The car in front of Evan was barely going the speed limit, so Evan passed the car leaving only two cars between him and Nick's cycle. They climbed higher and higher on the highway weaving around the hairpin turns. Barely room for two cars on the roadway—one coming, one going in the opposite direction and minimal shoulder to speak of. A steady stream of traffic moved in the opposite direction, perhaps returning beachgoers who got caught in the storm.

Evan's car began to fog up from the humidity. He fumbled for the defrost switch to get the fog off the windshield. He used his hand to clear a visual pathway. Inadvertently, he hit the air conditioning button, which helped. He couldn't find the defrost button in the dark and was driving too fast to fiddle with the overhead lights. Nick passed another car, giving Evan three cars behind to catch up. Since they were on the winding Tramuntana, he assumed Nick was going to the hotel. Maybe he thought Nick was going to hide there or perhaps outrun him. The car in front of Evan turned off at a lookout point, not that there was anything to see in the rain, but the driver obviously got tired of being tailgated. Now, only two cars remained between Nick and Evan as he wiped the sweat off his brow. He crept closer to the car in front of him and honked, the rude noise was so loud it scared him, and the driver in front of him shook his fist. So much for trying to get the car in front of him to pull over.

The car in front of him did the opposite—he slowed down. Evan quickly passed going uphill and barely got back into his lane of traffic before another car came downhill in the opposite lane. Evan shivered in the car with the A/C blowing on max air, but it wasn't something he could finger at the speed they were going. He hit the gas pedal and pulled out to pass the car in front of him. The driver, probably very annoyed, backed off and let Evan pass. Evan signaled a handwave of thanks and buzzed around the car. Now there was only one car in front of him and behind Nick as they took the steep turns at breakneck speed. Trucks were coming down in the opposite lane of traffic making it difficult to pass. Passing on an uphill climb was seriously dangerous anytime, not to mention the wet weather conditions and slippery pavement.

Evan pulled out to pass and had to duck back in again because of a car coming from the opposite direction. He waited, pulled out again and sped up to pass— he was finally behind Nick. Sweat dripped down Evan's back. The wipers rubbed on the window shield, scraping hard against the glass. There were no other cars in front of Nick, so he sped up. Evan pushed the gas and considered banging into Nick, forcing him off the road. He quickly glanced at the speed—50 mph. on a road with steep cliffs on either side. When he looked up, Nick had turned his head back over his shoulder and waived something at him—a gun. Evan's instinct was to duck his head toward the steering wheel. The bullet cracked a hole in the glass in the center of the windshield and shot through the car. Nick rapidly turned around again, pulled forward to pass a truck in his lane and didn't see a huge truck coming downhill from the opposite direction. The truck slammed into Nick and knocked him off his motorcycle and rolled over him. The motorcycle bounced up against the grill, crumbling the metal into twisted scrap.

Evan could see the driver of the truck in the downward lane was losing control and heading toward him. Some dark objects flew across the windshield. In that moment, Evan knew that the driver of the wayward truck was going to crash into him. He released the seatbelt, jerked his car rapidly to the left, took his foot off the gas, opened the car door and fell out and rolled on his shoulder and knees in the gravel while his car flew over the embankment, tumbled end over front, bounced off the cliff and landed on a massive boulder—then BAM! An explosion created a fireball so large it shot to the sky with plumes of heavy black smoke. The truck continued crossing over to the right lane, toppled sideways spilling avocados on the highway and over the cliff.

Evan felt himself grabbing on to tree roots in the dark, straining to keep from falling over the cliff. He tried to hoist a leg to heave himself back onto the pavement and pulled back on the tree roots for leverage—but then the tree roots gave way, sending Evan head over heels backwards down the cliff. He bounced off of rocks, hit another tree on the way down, rolled on his back, then over his head with a speed he could not stop. He tried grabbing brush while he was rolling but couldn't get ahold of anything stationary. Something stabbed him in the back, and he felt his pants tear, his shirt rip from his torso. Sharp rocks cut into him while he was tumbling. He landed hard on sand and rocks and felt something snap in his leg, like the sound of baseball bat cracking—a loud pop. He could feel blood oozing from his head but he couldn't move.

He lay there in a heap, thinking he was not dead but probably would be...then everything went black.

CHAPTER 41
Danielle

It was nearly midnight when Danielle woke up from a bad dream. She felt she had been tumbling aimlessly through space. It made her feel unsettled. The bedroom was dark with only a dim light illuminating the hallway on the way to Trevor's bedroom. She sat up, turned on a lamp, grabbed her fleece bathrobe and walked down the hall to check on him. He was sleeping soundly and looked adorable with his long eyelashes and thumb in his mouth. She adjusted his blanket and covered him up a bit more.

Although she didn't usually wake up in the middle of the night, she felt hungry and wandered to the kitchen. What to eat? Her favorite was peanut butter and jelly, so she made a sandwich, ate it, drank a glass of milk and walked back to bed, hoping she'd be able to sleep. Evan's call made her feel hopeful—excited that he would be coming home. It would be such a relief not to have to worry about him anymore. They'd never been apart this long, and now that she was married with a child, she no longer liked being alone. She climbed back into bed, turned off the light and felt like she would be able to sleep until morning. Evan had promised to call her with the flight information so she could pick him up at the airport. She pulled the duvet cover around her shoulders, nestled into her pillow and took a deep breath. In no time, she was asleep.

The sound of Trevor crying woke her up. She wiped the sleep out of her eyes and glanced at the clock. Nearly noon. She'd overslept. No wonder Trevor was crying. He had pulled himself up on the bed rail and was standing there, his face blotchy from crying and put his arms out to her like an abandoned child whose mother hadn't fed him. Guilt consumed her for sleeping so late, so she picked him up, soothed his face with a kiss, rubbed his back and took him into the kitchen.

While she made breakfast for Trevor, she wondered why she hadn't heard from Evan. She put Trevor in his highchair, gave him some applesauce and cooked oatmeal and reached for her purse to pull out her cell phone. She dialed Evan. He didn't answer. What was going on? She tried again to no avail. Maybe he was in his room in the shower. She decided he must have bumped his ring-tone to the off position on his iPhone and that's why it wasn't ringing. When Trevor was finished with breakfast, she picked him up, changed his diaper which she should have done before breakfast, but he was so hungry she did it out of sequence. He giggled at her and she tickled him on each side of his face which made him smile. How much she loved him was hard to explain. It seemed years ago that she was single, and now was married to a man she loved with all her heart, with a baby they had created, a joyous feeling of overwhelming gratitude. She put on a clean outfit for Trevor and set him in his playpen with his favorite soft toys, a bunny and a teddy bear.

With Trevor settled, she grabbed her cell phone and called Evan again. No answer. What the hell? Why couldn't she reach Evan? She decided to call the *Calatrava* hotel and ask them to put a call to his room. She waited. The hotel room's phone rang but no one answered it. Danielle had chills as she pondered what was wrong. She dialed the hotel again. "Do you think you could send someone up to his room? I've tried to reach him on his cell phone several times, and I can't. You connected me to his room and there's no answer. I'm worried something has happened."

The reception desk said they would send someone up to his room. Danielle said she'd wait on the line. It seemed to take forever, but she remembered their room had been on the fifteenth floor and the elevators took time to get there. She took a deep breath and nervously twisted her auburn hair into a curl around her fingers.

"Mrs. Wentworth?"

"Yes? I'm here."

"We knocked on the door, there was no answer nor was there a *"do not disturb"* sign on the door. We opened the room. The bed has not been slept in, but there are still clothes in the closet."

"Oh. Well, some of the clothes are still mine. It's a long story. My husband was going to book a flight home today and call me with the information so I could pick him up."

"Do you want us to leave a message for him?"

"Yes, please. Tell him to call me as soon as possible."

Danielle hung up and stood in the kitchen unable to move. Her hands felt clammy. This wasn't like Evan. When he said he was going to do something, he did it. Probably the former cop in him, he was true to his word. She considered what might have happened. Maybe he had difficulty getting a flight, or perhaps he went down to the dining room for a late breakfast or lunch. She checked her cell phone for any messages—nothing. Her cell phone rang in her hand, jolting her a bit.

"Hello? Evan?"

"Is this Mrs. Wentworth?"

"Yes. Who is this?"

"This is Police Sgt. Sandoval. I'm calling from Mallorca."

Danielle felt a chill from her neck to her feet. "Is something wrong?"

"I'm afraid there's been an accident."

"Oh no, no, no." Danielle stopped breathing and grabbed the side of the kitchen table for support.

"Ma'am, are you still there?"

Danielle's knees felt like liquid unable to support her. "Is Evan all right?

"Mrs. Wentworth, there's been an accident up in the mountains. I'm sorry to inform you your husband was killed in a car accident."

"This can't be true! He had just called me last night. He was booking a flight to come home today. Are you sure?"

"Yes, Ma'am. We found his wallet at the scene."

"What scene?" Danielle felt faint and sat down at the kitchen table.

"A truck hit a motorcyclist who was killed instantly. The truck driver tried to avoid going over the cliff and toppled over. We believe your husband tried to avoid the collision and his car went off the cliff."

Danielle had no idea what the police sergeant said after that. All the blood drained from her face and she slunk off the chair to the floor in a heap. When she awoke, she was disoriented as if she was coming out of a very bad nightmare. She sat up and realized she had fainted. The room was still spinning. Nausea overcame her and she vomited. Her whole body started shaking. Evan had been in an accident and he was dead—this couldn't be happening.

CHAPTER 42
Danielle and Marie

Weak with nausea and panic, Danielle called her mother, Marie.

"Mama—" and then her frail voice broke with sobbing tears.

"What's wrong, Danielle? Is Trevor okay?"

"Trevor's fine." Danielle choked out the words. "Evan's dead."

"Oh my God, no! What happened?"

"There was an accident on the road up in the mountains. A truck over turned and Evan avoided the truck and went off a cliff."

"How do you know this?"

"A police sergeant called me. He found Evan's wallet at the scene."

"I'm confused. I thought Evan was booking a flight home."

"He was coming home. I don't know why he was traveling up in the mountains the night before. He never called me with his return flight information.

I tried to reach him on his cell phone twice. He didn't pick up. That's not like him."

"Honey, I'm so sorry. You stay put, I'm coming right over."

"Mama, I don't know what to do."

"We'll figure it out together."

Danielle hung up the phone and sat down in a chair. Her body felt heavy, as if someone put a huge sack of rocks on her back. There was nothing she could do but wait for her mom. Evan's death seemed like a very bad nightmare that she couldn't wake up from—her worst fear of Evan being on Mallorca intent on finding Ryan. He had told her he couldn't find Ryan, was giving up on his plan to find justice and was coming home. What had happened between the phone call he made to her, and his being up on the Tramuntana mountains? Did he intend to make one last drive to the hotel *Cielo*? Had someone given him information about Ryan? The police sergeant didn't say who was killed in the accident besides Evan and the truck driver. He did say it was someone on a motorcycle. Danielle rubbed her swollen eyes, went to pick up Trevor out of his playpen and sat on the sofa waiting for her mother. Trevor sat on her lap as she cried softly…an ache so painful in her chest it made it hard to breathe. She thought she'd never recover from the loss. She rocked Trevor back and forth knowing that Evan wouldn't see his son grow up, would never see him play sports, graduate from school, get married—they would never have any grandchildren. Overnight, she was a widow. Her worst fear had become a reality.

The doorbell rang and jarred her out of her grief. She carried Trevor on her hip and opened the door. Marie entered, put her arms around her oldest daughter and Trevor. Together they moved toward the sofa and sat down. Marie put Trevor in his playpen. He looked perplexed, as if he knew something was very wrong. Danielle had not cried before in front of

Trevor, at least not to the extent she was crying now, unable to stop. She blew her nose and sat with her hands limply on her lap and felt like she was five years old incapable of managing anything.

"I've called Dad at work, and Chloe. Lena and Lucas are coming over later. Everyone wants to provide support and help you in any way they can. Dad's just devastated."

Danielle sat up straight, wiped her eyes and stared into space. "I want to see where the accident happened," she stated as a definitive decision.

Marie raise her eyebrows. "You want to go to Mallorca?"

"I have to see the accident for myself."

Marie reached out her hand and put it on her daughter's shoulder. "I don't think that's a good idea. I think we should contact the policeman who called you, find out who the coroner is and have the body shipped back here. That way we can have a celebration of life for family and close friends. Do you have the phone number for Sgt. Sandoval?"

"I don't. Could you call the Mallorca police and ask for him?"

Marie took the phone, called information and then dialed the Palma Mallorca police station and asked for Sgt. Sandoval. Marie waited while the phone rang.

"Hello. This is Marie DuBois. My son-in-law was killed yesterday in Mallorca in a car crash in the mountains. I'm looking for Sgt. Sandoval who contacted my daughter about Evan Wentworth's death. Can you give me his number?"

Danielle sat numbly on the sofa. All energy had drained from her body.

Marie grabbed for a pencil and paper in her purse and waited. The man who answered the phone gave her Sgt. Sandoval's phone number. Marie wrote it down and then dialed. "Sgt. Sandoval?"

"Yes."

"This is Marie DuBois. You called my daughter, Danielle Wentworth about the death of her husband, Evan, yesterday. He was killed in a car crash on Mallorca."

"Yes, Ma'am. How can I help you?"

"We'd like to have the body flown back to St. Paul-de-Vence where he lives."

Sgt. Sandoval coughed trying to get the words out. "I don't think that will be possible."

"What do you mean, not possible?"

"There's no body. His car went over the cliff and exploded upon impact. The fire from the explosion consumed the car. It's so far down the cliff, we can't even reach it."

Marie gasped and put her hand to her mouth in horror.

"Are you still there?" Sgt. Sandoval asked.

"Yes. I understand." Marie said. "Thank you for giving me that information."

"I'm terribly sorry for your loss." Sgt. Sandoval said.

"I'll need a death certificate."

"Yes, of course. Give me your address and I'll pass that information on to the coroner."

Marie clicked off her phone and bit her lips as she sat down, distraught as to how she would tell Danielle the news without breaking down herself.

The doorbell rang again. Marie got up to answer the door and let Chloe, Lena, and Lucas, Danielle's sisters and brother, into the living room. Chloe was crying, Lena was shaking and Lucas immediately went to his Danielle and engulfed her in a hug. They all sat numbly in the living room, not sure what to say.

Marie decided she had to be honest with Danielle. What purpose would it serve if she sugar-coated the reality?

"Danielle, when Evan's car went over the cliff, it exploded upon impact—there is no body to retrieve."

Danielle put her hands to her face, bent over and wailed. Chloe put her arms around her fragile sister, her heart breaking for her. No words were enough to take away the deep grief she knew Danielle was feeling.

Lena went into the kitchen to make some sandwiches for everyone hoping Danielle would eat something.

The doorbell rang again, but the door was ajar, so Gaspard let himself in.

Danielle looked up at her father, ran to him and cried in his arms. Gaspard held her tightly while he soothed her back with soft rubs. "I'm so sorry, honey."

Marie filled Gaspard in on the details while Lena returned with turkey, lettuce and tomato sandwiches. Lena offered Danielle a sandwich. Danielle shook her head. "I'm not hungry."

"I know you're not hungry, but try to eat something," Marie offered.

Danielle reluctantly took a half-sandwich and set the plate on the table in front of the sofa.

Suddenly Danielle sat up erect on the sofa with a determined look on her face. "I don't believe Evan's dead."

Marie sighed and turned to Danielle and put her hand on her daughter's shoulder. "Honey, you're in shock. He is dead. It's a terrible tragedy we all have to accept."

Danielle bit her upper lip. "I'll believe it when I see where the accident happened. What if he fell down the cliff before the car went over? I have to go to Mallorca."

Gaspard looked at his wife and shook his head indicating she should let their daughter talk, then added, "I wonder if they did any search and rescue?"

"That's a great idea. We can contact the police and ask them if that's been done," Lucas said. "With how you described the terrain there, Danielle, one would think hikers and rock climbers could fall. They must have search and rescue teams on the island."

Gaspard offered, "I'll contact them in the morning. Whatever it costs, we can afford it."

Everyone sat silently, eating sandwiches except Danielle who took two bites and left the food on her plate.

Trevor awoke in his playpen, startled by the room full of people. Marie picked him up and he settled down on her lap, then wiggled so much she put him on the floor. "I'll stay with Danielle tonight," Marie said affirmatively to her family. "I don't want you to be alone, honey."

Danielle nodded. "I'd appreciate that."

Gaspard, Lucas, Lena and Chloe got up to leave and alternatively gave Danielle supportive hugs.

"I'll talk to you after I speak with the police in the morning." Gaspard said.

Gaspard kissed Danielle on the forehead. Tears brimmed in her eyes.

Danielle turned toward her mother. "I know you don't want me to look into Evan's death, but I have to. A slim thread of hope is better than no hope at all.

When I'm sure he's not alive, then and only then will I accept his death.

Marie embraced her daughter. "I think it will be emotionally exhausting to visit the site where the accident happened, but I will support you in any way I can. Let's hope Dad can find out if a helicopter can search the area where Evan's car went over the cliff. I just realized I should call Evan's parents. They will be devastated to hear about Evan's accident. I'm sure the police had no information on their whereabouts. With the time zone difference, I'll contact them tomorrow.

It breaks my heart to have to make this phone call to them.

CHAPTER 43
Evan

Water splashed in his face jolting him awake. He stared at the sky. Seagulls flew overhead swooping and coasting on air currents. He tilted his head toward the sea. Waves formed, crested and rolled into shore. His mouth felt dry. He licked his parched lips. Where was he? Then, he remembered. The accident. The nightmare of going over the cliff. By the grace of God he was still alive. Could he sit up?

He pushed his arms and hands into the sand to an upright position and groaned with the pain in his back. Once sitting, he noticed his torn slacks and a gouge in his leg. A broken femur? Could he get up on one leg and stand? No. There was nothing to hold on to. Although he was sitting in the sun, he shivered. His clothes were soaked from the sea water that had come in with the tide. Thank God he was far enough in the cove, or he would have drowned.

He noticed he only had on one shoe—the other must have ripped off during the fall. His side hurt and so did the back of his head. He reached his right arm behind his head and felt the bump which was the size of an orange. Blood had crusted on the front of his head as he felt around a wound. His side ached. Most likely he'd bruised or broken a rib or two. With his bare foot he pushed off the other shoe. It toppled over in the sand. He reached over for the shoe, shook out the sand then took out the shoe laces. His leg had stopped bleeding but he wanted to stabilize the bone. Frustrated, he pulled off his t-shirt, bit it with his teeth and tore the fabric. With both hands, he tore strips. One long strip he put around his forehead and tied it with a knot at the back of his head. Did he have a concussion? Probably. He felt dizzy. With the other ragged strips, he wrapped them around his leg and tied the fabric in place with the shoestrings he knotted together.

Thirst overcame him. All that water in the sea and nothing to drink. He heard water running. What was that? Turning on his side, he surveyed his surroundings. He was in a cove with cliffs on either side—massive sloping cliffs of brush, trees and rock. The entrance to the sea was narrow, allowing the tide to come in a night. Perhaps it was low tide or he would have drowned during the night, but the water had only doused him, not worse. Saltwater was probably good for his wounds.

He focused on the sound of running water and turned toward it. A waterfall cascading into the sand a short distance away. He spotted odd objects jutting out in the sand and thought they were rocks—perfectly formed oval shaped rocks that looked like avocados—a sign of delirium? He turned over on his good leg, pulled himself along keeping his wounded leg as stiff as possible and explored the odd-shaped items in the sand. Unbelievable. Avocados—several of them in the sand. He tore the skin off, bit into one and ate it voraciously, discarded the pit and grabbed another. How the avocados ended up in the sand seemed like a miracle. It was hot in the blazing sun. He needed to get to the waterfall. He knew he could live without food, but couldn't survive without water. Unable to crawl on his knees he turned over on his good side, kept his ankles together and dragged himself on his elbow a few inches at a time. The excruciating movements sent waves of pain throughout his lower extremity. Every muscle in his body ached. Even moving slowly was overwhelming. Exhausted, he stopped.

His head spun. Danielle. He was supposed to be on a flight home. Reaching in his back pocket he found his cell phone. It looked hopeless—completely bent and shattered. Nevertheless, he tried to turn on his phone. Nothing—no light, no tone. Useless.

He continued slithering along in the sand, resting every few feet. He finally made it to the waterfall, reached into the rock pool of water and cupped his hands. The water tasted so good. Once he was settled against a rock, he felt bruised and battered, but alive. He could survive on water and heaven-sent avocados, but who would know he was alive and how would anyone find him? At least he had water and was in the shade or he'd blister from being in the sun with his fair skin. However, he thought if he stayed in the shade and was not on the beach area of the cove, no one would see him. Perhaps if he crawled back to the sand near the opening of the cove, he could yell at any boats coming by. For now, he was too tired to do anything but rest.

He closed his eyes, listening to the roar of the surf. The accident played over in his mind, Nick shooting at him from his motorcycle and then watching Nick getting hurled in the air and being crushed under the on-coming truck. No doubt, Nick was dead. He couldn't have survived the impact. This was not the retribution Evan hoped for, but things didn't always turn out the way one wanted.

CHAPTER 44
Cassie

When Nick didn't return, Cassie turned on the television to watch the nightly news. She had a strange feeling something bad had happened. It made no sense that Nick had pushed her aside so violently she almost fell off the boat. Nick was being chased by some man yelling "I'm coming for you." What was that about?

She grabbed a soda from the refrigerator and settled on the sofa bench. She watched coverage of political issues, and then coverage of a horrific accident on the Tramuntana mountains—a collision of a truck and a motorcyclist who was pronounced dead at the scene. A wave of fear filled her. She dropped her soda can. It splashed and puddled on the floorboards creating a mess. Was Nick dead? Shivers of dread filled her. She got up, grabbed paper towels and began wiping up the floor while listening to the drone of a newscaster.

Reality set in. If Nick was alive, he would have returned to the boat, or he'd have called her to say he'd be late. Neither had happened. How would she know for sure if Nick was dead or alive?

The keys for the boat where on the counter. She grabbed the keys, then her purse with her car keys, locked the boat and headed to her car. The Palma police station was close by. She would ask them if they knew who was involved in the accident. Her hands shook as she drove through town worried about what she would learn from the police. She parked her car and ran into the police station. A policeman was at the front desk looking at a monitor. He looked up at her.

"Excuse me. I'm Cassandra Benoit. I just saw the news about a terrible motorcycle crash on the mountain highway. Can you tell me more information about who was involved? I think the motorcyclist is someone I know. In fact, I'm staying on his boat."

"Ms. Benoit, please have a seat. I'll see what I can find out for you."

Cassie paced the waiting room, picking on her thumb. Thoughts were scrambling through her mind so quickly she couldn't sort them out. If Nick was dead, what would she do?

She watched as a tall thin officer with grey hair walked down the hallway toward her. "I'm Officer Lopez. How can I help you?"

"I'm Cassandra Benoit. I saw the news about a motorcycle crash up on the Tramuntana—I think I might know the person involved in the accident. Can you tell me his name? Is he all right?"

A perplexed look crossed Officer Lopez's face. "Are you related?"

"No. I'm uh, the woman who was shot at the hotel *Cielo* a short time ago. I've been staying at Nick Fontaine's boat here in the marina while I recover. A man approached Nick earlier tonight, yelled something about coming after him, and Nick took off on his motorcycle."

"Why don't you come back to my office?" Officer Lopez indicated the way down the hall. Cassie took a deep breath and followed him. The overhead LED lights had a harsh glare giving the hallway a bleak greenish cast. Officer Lopez sat down at his cluttered desk. "Please, have a seat. Tell me again how you know Nick Fontaine?" Officer Lopez's dark eyes were inquisitive while he rubbed his chin.

"I hired Nick a short time ago. He was my construction foreman."

"I see." Lopez nodded.

Cassie bit the inside of her cheek. "Is he the motorcyclist who was in the accident?"

"We think so. It was a head-on collision. The truck driver and the motorcyclist didn't survive. Do you think you could identify the cyclist's body?"

Blood drained out of Cassie's face. She momentarily closed her eyes. "Where is the body?" Cassie asked.

"The ME is taking the body to the coroner and they're not at the morgue yet. Can you come by in the morning?"

"Oh, please no. I'll wait. I'm so upset. I want to get this over with as soon as possible. What made you think it was Nick Fontaine?" Cassie wondered.

"I met him a few weeks ago when there was an investigation for the murder of Chad Callahan, a boatmate of Mr. Fontaine's."

Cassie tilted her head and her eyes glanced up at the ceiling. "Yes, I remember Nick telling me about that murder. He didn't know Chad very well, and was shocked to learn he'd been killed."

"Do you know if Mr. Fontaine has any family?"

Cassie shook her head. "I'm sorry, I don't. I think he may have had a brother. I found a photograph on the boat but it's very confusing. Nick's face looks familiar but the names below the photograph are different. I'm not even sure Nick Fontaine is his real name. I was wondering since Nick is dead, what will happen with his boat?"

Officer Lopez leaned forward on his desk. "If there is no next of kin, we'd put the boat up for auction and sell it as is. You said you're staying on the boat now?"

"Yes. I couldn't face staying in my apartment alone. I've been afraid whoever shot me knew where I lived. When Nick invited me to stay on his boat, I accepted. He was very kind to me. I can't believe he's dead. You said he was killed on impact?"

"Yes, it appeared Mr. Fontaine was trying to pass a car and didn't see the truck coming from the opposite direction—one of the farm trucks tried to avoid him and tipped over on its side spilling avocados all over the roadway. The driver of the truck died in the hospital, and the driver of another car went off the cliff and died in an explosion."

"Oh, that's terrible. Nick left in such a rush and didn't have his helmet on."

Office Lopez shrugged his shoulders. "I don't think that would have made a difference. I would prepare yourself for a difficult identification. His body was badly mangled."

Tears run down Cassie's cheeks. She wiped them with her fingertips.

Officer Lopez leaned forward. "I'm sorry for your loss."

"Thank you. I relied on Nick so much to get the hotel completed, which it now is. I wanted to get back to work, but my shoulder is still sore.

"Have you learned anything about the motive and why I was shot?"

Cassie waited while Officer Lopez scrolled through his monitor. "According to Detective Brasco and Sgt. Sandoval who were handling your case, they've indicated there was a CI involved who learned what may have instigated the shooting."

"What's a CI?" Cassie asked.

"Confidential Informant. It appears one of your workers was at a bar bragging about his wages. He said you paid considerably more than most hotels on the island."

Cassie raised her eyebrows. "I asked workers what their hourly rate had been at other hotels. They told me what they had been making before," Cassie said defensively.

Officer Lopez leaned back in his chair so it rested on the back wall and folded his arms. "People don't always tell the truth. Because you were willing to pay what they asked, you took crews away from other hotels who were doing major renovations. I think you angered hotel owners who couldn't hold on to the only resources they had to get their work accomplished."

"I'm from Barcelona. I suppose I never thought to verify wages because it seemed in line what we paid in there."

"Yes, but Barcelona is a much larger city."

Embarrassed, Cassie pursed her lips and nodded. "While I'm here, do you know who shot me?"

Office Lopez scrolled through his monitor. "Detective Brasco indicates it was a gang leader, a mercenary, who wanted to scare you into going back to Barcelona. If your hotel didn't open, they hoped they would be able to get their workers to come back to the jobs they had before."

"Do you think I'm safe now? I've built this beautiful hotel and wanted to open it soon, but I need reassurance someone's not going to try to kill me."

"The gang leader has been arrested. He'll be tried on attempted murder. You don't have to worry about being shot again. If you adjust your wages to the going rate, I don't think there will be any future problems. You might meet with some of the hotel owners and get wage rates for bellmen, concierge, maids, and whatever help you need in the future. If the wages are fair, people can choose who they want to work for."

"Thank you for that. My father, Roberto, runs Benoit Construction in Barcelona. He was devastated to learn I'd been shot. He thought this was a friendly island of helpful people."

"We are a friendly island, but we struggle with the economy. There are just so many workers to handle all the jobs available. Some workers move back and forth between Mallorca, Menorca and Formentera—even Ibiza. A good job with higher wages in the hotel industry is hard to find. When there is work that pays considerably above the going pay scale, people then flock to that location. It's how we try to keep a balance—pay the same for skills, and let workers decide where they want to work."

"Understood. I never meant to cause so much disruption."

"You're lucky to still be alive."

Cassie bit her upper lip. "I know. It's all been very traumatic."

Officer Lopez rose. "Are you okay about waiting in the front office? It might be another hour before the body arrives at the morgue."

"Yes, sure. Tell you what. I'll wait in my car in the parking lot. I can rest. Just knock on the window when the coroner has arrived."

Office Lopez walked Cassie to the front door, then turned and went back inside.

Cassie opened her car door, sat inside feeling emotionally trampled. Not only was Nick dead, but she had made a major error in paying her workers far more than they had been making on other jobs. She thought of her time with Nick. The work he had done was flawless and appreciated. She remembered his kiss on her lips. What would she do without him? Tears ran down her cheeks. Her heart ached. Even if Nick was not who he said he was, she was very fond of him, perhaps even more than fond. The future felt like a bad omen. How would she face identifying Nick's body?

CHAPTER 45
Gaspard, Danielle and Marie

The next morning Gaspard rang Danielle on her cell phone. On the third ring she picked up.

"Hi, Dad. What did you learn?"

"I was able to convince the police I needed a helicopter to scan the area where Evan went over the cliff. It's a copter used for medical flights."

Danielle sat down on the edge of her bed. "What does that mean?"

"If Evan is alive, the EC145 has a portable intensive-care transport respirator, a bi-phase defibrillator and multi-functioning monitoring. They can treat someone in-flight to the hospital."

Danielle breathed a sigh of relief. "That sounds so hopeful. If they found him injured, but alive, would they take him to a hospital there?"

"Yes, probably. That depends on his condition. He might need to be transported by air ambulance back to Nice. But, remember, honey, we don't even know if he's alive."

"I know, Dad. I have to be hopeful. It's a small thread, but a thread and I'm hanging on to it. When do you leave?"

"Later this afternoon. We'll do the search tomorrow."

"What's this going to cost?"

"Don't worry about it. It was expensive, but I know you need to have resolution. We all love Evan very much and hope that he somehow survived, but you have to be prepared. It might not be possible."

"I know, Dad. When I go to sleep at night, it's like I feel him talking to me as if he were still alive. Are you sure I can't come along?"

"No, honey. It's really crowded in those copters with all the equipment. Only room for the pilot, one other medic and myself. I promise I'll let you know if we find anything."

"Love you, Dad."

"Love you, too. Say some prayers. I'll be in touch."

Danielle clicked off her phone and sat on the edge of the bed. Marie came into the bedroom. "Was that Dad?"

"Yes. He's leaving for Mallorca this afternoon. They're doing a search tomorrow. Will you stay with me? I don't want to be alone."

Marie nodded. "Sure. I don't want you to be alone either. What did he say?"

"He's hired a medical helicopter of some sort to scan the area where the accident occurred. I wanted to go with him, but he said there wasn't room in the helicopter for me—just room for the pilot, a medical EMT and himself."

"I'm sure he'll let us know if he finds anything."

"This is going to be the longest wait—I won't be able to sleep tonight."

Marie nodded. "The weather is nice. Why don't we take Trevor for a stroll? It would do you good to get some fresh air. You look pale and fragile. I'm making you some hearty chicken soup when we get back. I noticed you had some chicken thighs in the refrigerator, that will go to waste if they are not used soon. The soup will do you good."

"Yes, Mama. Your soup is very welcome." Danielle walked over to her mother. "Thanks for staying with me. It's so much easier to take care of Trevor when you're around. He wants to walk by himself on those wobbly legs."

Danielle put a fresh shirt and leggings on Trevor and tossed a blanket in the stroller. He loved getting outside in the fresh air and sunshine. Marie and Danielle walked down the hill past flowering white and deep burgundy petunias and thick bushes of pink scatter roses. Gravel cracked under the carriage. The sun felt warm, healing and invigorating. Trevor sat in the walker pointing at bunnies and birds trying to make sounds that reflected what he was seeing. A neighbor's dog, a friendly golden retriever, padded toward them for a greeting and rubbed his flank against their knees. Trevor giggled at the dog who came over to the stroller and stuck his head inside, giving him sloppy kisses and making Trevor laugh. When he laughed, they all laughed and it felt good to escape, even for the moment, to a place of happiness without stress or depressing thoughts. They walked for over an hour with the sun blazing down on their heads and shoulders, the soft breezes in the air caressing their faces. As they headed back up the hill, Marie said, "This is such a beautiful house Evan bought for you. I've always loved the long bright blue shutters, and the climbing jasmine gently winding around the windows complimenting grey shades of the stone. The fountain in your front yard is so welcoming for so many different birds, finches, woodpeckers and doves. I enjoy visiting you here."

Danielle's face went from a smile to biting her lips with tears washing over her cheeks. "It's our home. It wouldn't be the same without Evan. I don't think I could live here alone...it would be too big for Trevor and me...too many memories." Danielle started to hiccup which was something she did when she was crying or nervous.

"Let's get you both inside so I can start the soup," Marie said.

Danielle nodded and wiped her tears away knowing she had to be brave for at least another day.

CHAPTER 46
Evan

Evan awoke with his mouth tasting of grit and seawater. He'd covered himself at night with sand that undoubtedly blew into his face while he slept. He sat up brushing the mess from his chest, hair and arms. Another hot sunny day stuck on this island with no way to let anyone know he was alive. He glanced toward the cliff on one side of the cove and noticed something gleaming on the beach. Obviously not another avocado, but something shining. Could he get to it? The pain wracking his body had lessened, but his muscles were weak from immobility. No more avocados had appeared and he was ravenous, feeling weak with a sense of panic about not having any food. He inched up to the rock pond and put his face into the water, drinking all that he could manage without choking. The back of his head hurt less, but he felt weary and dizzy from lack of food.

He turned toward the shiny object in the beach. Could he slither over to it, and would it be worth the effort? He convinced himself that moving, albeit slowly and painstakingly, was better off than staying immobile. It gave him greater appreciation for those in the war who lost limbs, those who could not move if they wanted to. With the fractured or broken leg resting on top of his good leg, he inched his way on the beach toward the glare of the object. After what seemed like an hour, he was now near enough to make out what it was. A mirror of some sort. He let out a whoop. It was a red sideview mirror from a car. With a mirror he'd have something to use as a reflector from the sun. Was it possible when his rental car exploded and the mirror tumbled landing in the sand? He accelerated crawling on his side. Although the mirror was cracked, it was still usable. How many movies had he seen where a mirror was used to signal help?

He grabbed the mirror, slithered back to where he started and found a place in the sand where he could gouge out SOS should there be an airplane overhead. It surprised him that he hadn't seen any aircraft, but then again, he was nowhere near an airport. Perhaps he could signal a boat, but he hadn't seen any boats since his accident. He lay on his side and marked the letter S, then moved sideways to mark the O, and then carved the S. Exhausted and sunburned, he dragged the mirror with one hand back to the area where he had been sitting in the shade. He didn't think he could make it, felt like he was passing out, but he thought of Danielle, then Trevor, and slithered forward again on one side. He held the mirror directly into the sun, thankful the sun was out to reflect the rays back to the sky. If only someone, anyone, would appear near the cove. The waves with large whitecaps were wild from the wind. He focused the mirror on his chest and was determined to keep inching every hour or so toward the sun. Surely someone would see the reflection. Tears brimmed in his eyes. "Dammit," he said. "I don't want to die."

CHAPTER 47
Gaspard

He took a taxi to the air ambulance helicopter rental facility and was surprised by the number of copters available for rent in emergencies. He thanked the taxi driver, grabbed his suitcase and went inside the huge hanger with the door open. "Hello, I'm Gaspard DuBois. I've rented a copter to look for my son-in-law whose car went off the cliff up in the mountains."

"Yes, hello. I'm Javier, the pilot. I'll be taking you up. This is Miguel, the EMT, who will be assisting me."

Gaspard shook hands with each of the men. "Do you think I could leave my suitcase here while we go up? I'm hoping to check into the hotel where Evan was staying. Do you know where the accident occurred?"

"Yes, Javier said, brushing his dark hair off of his forehead. "There's a map on the wall over here. Let me show you where we're headed. Have you been to Mallorca before?"

"No, sorry. I live in St. Paul-de-Vence. My daughter and her husband were here on a vacation, a belated honeymoon.

"Was your daughter involved in the accident?"

Gaspard winced. "No, she had returned home, uh, to take care of the baby. It's a long story."

Javier pointed to the location of the accident on the map which showed the mountain range of the Serra de Tramuntana. "It should only take us about a half-hour to get there. Do you get air sick?"

Gaspard shook his head. "No. I'll be fine. I run a company that charters yachts. We're on the sea a great deal, often in rough waters. Nothing bothers me."

"We have some paperwork for you to sign first, and we require a deposit as we discussed on the phone. The balance of the flight expense can be paid after we complete the search."

"That's fine," Gaspard agreed. "Since this isn't a search and rescue helicopter, do you have a SAR basket in case Evan is alive but seriously injured?"

"We've added a basket if it's needed."

Gaspard hastily wrote out a check for the deposit and signed all the release of liability forms while he heard the helicopter blades whirling in the background.

Gaspard followed Javier and Miguel to the copter, climbed in and settled in a seat. The copter lifted off creating a cloud of dust and then banked a hard left toward the mountains. They flew over Palma and headed toward the sea.

"Beautiful country," Gaspard shouted to Miguel who nodded in agreement. It was too noisy in the copter to carry on a conversation, so Gaspard concentrated on the mountains, anxious to fly over the terrain where the accident had occurred. He reached for his cell phone to take pictures if, in fact, there was something he would want to show Danielle, but if the wreckage was nothing but a pile of burnt metal, he was not willing to add to her grief by showing her horrific photos.

The copter continued to rise, lifting gracefully over the mountain ridges, caverns and beaches. It was surprisingly windy at this higher elevation making the copter pitch sideways. Javier yelled, "We're reaching the accident area— look to your right past the cove. You should see a badly burnt automobile."

Gaspard stretched his neck and leaned against the copter window looking straight down while the copter took a swerving dive to the right. He spotted the wreckage, what there was of it, and shuddered. From the looks of the explosion, there didn't seem to be any chance Evan could have survived the crash. He felt the blood drain from his face.

Miguel tapped Gaspard on the shoulder. "I don't see a survivor."

Gaspard nodded. "Do you think we could take the copter up to where the car went off the road?" Miguel hollered the request to Javier. They took a swooping dip to the right and climbed up to the Tramuntana highway. Circling around the area the copter dipped sharply to the left heading back out to sea. Gaspard had an overwhelming sense of loss and heartbreak for his daughter and their entire family. Evan was so young. What happened to cause his car to go over the cliff? And what was he doing on the highway the night before he was going to book a flight to return home? It didn't make sense. Evan was a responsible person who didn't take unnecessary risks. Perhaps, because Evan was planning on leaving Mallorca the next day, he chose to take one last drive up the mountains and the east coast. He wished he had an explanation that led to Evan's death.

"Do you think we could take one more pass over the car?"

Miguel relayed the information to Javier who nodded affirmatively.

The copter banked a left turn and dipped toward the accident area. Dejected, Gaspard took out his iPhone and readied it to take a few photos. If Danielle begged him, he would show them to her, heartbreaking as it would be. Since she wanted to come along and see for herself, she'd never forgive him if he didn't take pictures of where Evan died.

The copter dipped and swerved over the wreckage. Gaspard took several photos. As the copter turned, Gaspard noticed something in the cove they flew over. "Wait, go back, please!"

"What did you see?" Miguel asked.

"In that cove—something. I saw an SOS in the sand."

Javier hollered. "We'll try a fly-over, but I can't get too close. There's a headwind forcing us toward the cliffs."

Gaspard bit his upper lip and nervously rubbed his thick mustache. As the copter dipped closer to the sandy beach cove, he noticed a clearly gouged out SOS in the sand. "Can you get closer to the inside of the cove?" Gaspard asked. Then he saw a glare coming from the cove, a blinding ray of the sun hitting a mirror. "There!" Gaspard shouted—there in the sand behind the cliff entrance. I see a body!"

CHAPTER 48
Gaspard

He felt a rush of adrenaline once he spotted the body. Could it be Evan? As the copter circled around the area, he was more than hopeful. Gaspard shouted to Javier, "Can you land somewhere near in the sand?"

"No, the cove entrance is too small, however I can hover and send Miguel down with the basket."

Miguel opened the door and began readying himself to descend to the beach. The wench started unfurling and the basket was lowered slowly to the sandy area. Miguel hung on the wench coil wrapped around himself and clipped to his waist belt. The copter tilted to the right and Gaspard leaned out of the door anxious to see if the body was Evan's. When Miguel landed in the sand with the basket and medical supplies, Gaspard held his breath in anticipation. He watched Miguel approach the body—a badly sunburnt torso and waited. "He's alive!" Miguel yelled from the ground, but with the noise of the copter blades, it was hard for Gaspard to understand. Javier did an amazing job of hovering and holding the copter still.

Miguel attended to the limp body in the sand. "Do you know who you are?"

"Yes, Evan—Evan Wentworth."

Miguel asked, "Where do you hurt?"

"My leg—I think it's broken."

"Do you think you can sit up so I can hoist you into the basket?"

"Yes, but I'm feeling very weak."

"I'll help you." Miguel put his arm around Evan's back and lifted him into the basket and gave a thumbs up for the wench to take the basket up to the copter.

Gaspard was so nervous, he nearly bit his thumbnail in two. He watched the basket rising to the copter, dumbfounded Evan was still alive, badly sunburned, but alive. Javier yelled to Gaspard, "Grab the basket when it reaches the door opening and pull it in. Be careful not to lose your footing. The copter will tilt toward the weight coming into the door. Then unhook it and get the basket free so I can lower the wench and pull up Miguel."

Once Miguel strapped himself around his back and buttocks onto the wench, Javier began to pull him up easily. When the basket was level with the copter door Gaspard grabbed the wire side and pulled the basket in, careful not to fall out. The copter swerved back and forth, but stayed at the same altitude.

Gaspard reached into the basket for Evan's hand. Evan shook his head. "I can't believe you found me. I'd all but given up hope of being rescued because no one knew I was alive."

"You can thank Danielle. She was determined to search the area because she refused to believe you were dead."

Miguel was now at the door, and Javier instructed Gaspard to pull him in and undo the wench.

Gaspard said, "I saw the SOS in the sand, but how did you survive the car crash?"

Evan coughed and swallowed. "I opened the car door just before it went off the cliff. There were tree roots to hang onto until they gave away, sending me down these embankments. I smashed my phone. It's inoperable. I couldn't call for help. How long was I missing?"

"Several days."

"I lost all sense of time. I thought I would die out there on the sand. If it weren't for some avocados that washed up on the beach, I wouldn't have had any food—and the waterfall, it provided me with water to drink."

Miguel took Evan's vitals. "Heart rate is good, although weak. Some second and possible third degree burns on your torso and a number of gashes and bruises on your chest. Also, a nasty bump on your head."

Miguel hooked up a drip line to Evan's arm. "We'll get you to the local hospital so you can recover. I think if you had gone one or two more days, you wouldn't have survived."

Gaspard took out his cell phone and dialed Danielle. She picked up on the third ring. "Dad?"

"It's me, honey. I have good news." He handed his phone to Evan.

Evan choked up and tears began to form in his eyes. "Danielle? I'm alive."

Danielle gasped and squealed, "Oh my God! I just knew you weren't dead because I felt in my heart you were alive."

"They're taking me to the hospital. I'll call you after I'm settled."

"I love you so much, Evan. This is the best day of my life."

Evan handed the phone back to Gaspard. "He's very sunburned, bruised and thin, but otherwise he's doing very well. He has a fractured or broken leg, so the hospital is the best place for him. Will give you an update once the doctors have a chance to examine him." Gaspard could hear Danielle crying tears of relief. "Call your mother, and Kelly, will you?"

Danielle responded, "Of course. I'll tell everyone he's alive!"

CHAPTER 49
Cassie

Identifying Nick's body was brutal. His mangled blue-white arms and legs made Cassie want to wretch. But she understood she was the only person who could identify Nick. She nodded to the ME that she was finished and left the morgue. When she got back to her car, her resolve disappeared and she couldn't stop the angst or the tears of grief. With Nick dead, she realized she could no longer stay on his boat. She decided to gather her things, lock up the boat and return the keys to the police. Her cell phone pinged. She pulled over to the side of the road to answer the call from her father. "Hello, Dad. How are you?"

"I'm good. I've been worried about you. I called a couple of times, but got voicemail."

"Sorry. I've been busy at the morgue. With Nick dead, I don't know what I will do about scheduling a grand opening for the hotel."

"That's why I wanted to talk to you. I'm coming to Mallorca to help you run the hotel."

"Dad, that's really not necessary."

"You've been through a lot lately with a gunshot wound. I can turn the business over to Sebastian. He's more than capable of running the operation here. You deserve to feel safe and have some help with the logistics of planning a grand opening."

"Well, if you insist. I'd really appreciate your help. You can stay with me."

"I'll fly out tomorrow and call you later with my flight information. Pick me up from the airport?"

"Of course. Love you, Dad. Thanks for your support." Cassie sat in the car overwhelmed with gratitude. There was so much to organize for a grand opening. Having her father here to help with a myriad of details would so appreciated. She pushed her long dark hair behind her ears and wiped her mascara stained eye makeup off of her face, then headed to Nick's boat.

Cassie unlocked the boat's door, walked into the galley and sat down. It seemed unreal that Nick was dead—or whatever his real name was. A question that would never be answered after she found the photograph with two men, one obviously Nick, but with the name of Jed Reddiger. She opened a bottle of beer and sat on the deck one last time before packing her clothes. It was a warm humid night with a slight breeze. She sat cross-legged on a lounge chair and noticed the boat neighbor, Mrs. Delmonico, who Nick did not like, walking her dog heading in her direction. Cassie bent her head down as if interested in a spot on her capris. The little dog yapped as they got closer.

"Where's Nick?" Mrs. Delmonico questioned with pursed lips.

Cassie choked out the words. "He's dead."

Mrs. Delmonico's eyes widened. "I'm sorry, what did you say?"

"He's dead." Cassie's voice cracked in agony. "He was killed in a motorcycle crash up in the mountains."

Mrs. Delmonico twisted her lips, then bent over to pick up the dog and tuck it under her arm. Her unruly red hair flopped into her widened eyes. "Never liked Nick. He was a troublemaker in this marina, yelling all the time at Mr. Callahan, waking us all up at night with his accusations. Of course, Mr. Callahan, is now dead too."

"What does that have to do with anything?" Cassie snapped with a wild look in her eyes. She'd never encountered someone so rude, so obnoxious.

"Oh, nothing my dear. I'm just saying what I think. Why are you staying on Nick's boat if he's dead?"

"It's none of your business. I'm packing my things and will be leaving tonight."

"What's going to happen with Nick's boat?"

"The police will arrange to have it put up for auction."

Mrs. Delmonico rubbed her forehead. It was so peaceful around here before Nick arrived. Now we have a murder and motorcycle death—rather tragic in this small community."

Perturbed, Cassie stood up, grabbed her beer and said, "I have to go in and pack now. Have a pleasant evening." She turned, rolled her eyes and muttered under her breath as she walked into the galley, "Such a bitch."

CHAPTER 50
Danielle

"**M**om, Evan's alive!" Danielle hollered into the phone, wiping the happy tears gliding down her flushed cheeks.

Marie yelled, "Oh my God! It's a miracle. Where did they find him?"

"In a cove on the beach."

"Is he okay?"

Danielle heaved a huge sigh of relief. "Dad said he's fine, but has some serious gashes, bruises, a possible broken leg and is very sunburned."

Marie wondered, "I can't imagine how he stayed alive without water and food."

"He was near a waterfall according to Dad, and Evan had avocados to eat—so he did have some nourishment."

"Did you say avocados? That doesn't make any sense."

"I know. I'm sure Evan will explain it. For now, they are taking him to the hospital. I so want to fly there to be with Evan. If I can arrange a flight, could you watch Trevor?"

"Sure. If Evan needs surgery, he may not be able to come home for a while."

"I know. I called the *Calatrava*. His room is still available. I can pack up his clothing and stay in that room until he is ready to come home. Perhaps I can't do anything at the hospital, but I want to hold him in my arms. I can hardly believe he's alive."

"Understood. I'll tell Chloe and Lucas the wonderful news—they will be thrilled. Lena's been asking for a status update every few hours. It's been very stressful for the whole family. I'm so glad Dad was able to fly over the area where the accident occurred. It's unbelievable they found him considering his car exploded—I'm sorry, I shouldn't be bringing up these details—just nervous energy."

"It's okay, Mom. I am so filled with gratitude. I'll let you know what I can arrange for a flight. Do you want to pick Trevor up or do you want to stay here at the house with him?"

"I'll come and pick him up. With your younger brothers and sisters at home, and Dad still in Mallorca, it's easier for me to care for him at my house.

"Oh, yes, of course. I'm not thinking clearly right now. I'm so excited."

Marie added, "Call me when you have flight information and I'll pick up Trevor. There's never a day when I feel Trevor's a burden. He's one of the biggest joys in my life.

"Thanks, Mom."

Danielle ended the call and sat on the sofa, so full of nervous energy it made her feel like running a marathon. She walked outside on the patio and saw the sun setting with clouds turning a pale pink hue. Grateful tears starting flowing again. What looked like an angel was simply a cloud formation. Or was it?

CHAPTER 51
Danielle

Danielle contacted the hotel *Calatrava* and convinced the manager of the seemingly implausible story about her husband's accident and why he couldn't have possibly returned to his room for the past few days. They agreed to reduce the hotel charges, put her up in the same room so she could pack his things and her remaining items from her short time in the hotel room. She was pleased they were so understanding and accommodating.

She took a taxi to the hospital in Palma. Her heart was beating wildly in anticipation of seeing Evan.

"Excuse me. Can you tell me if Evan Wentworth is out of surgery?"

The charge nurse looked up from her computer screen. "Let me check for you. Ah, yes, he had surgery this morning."

"Can I see him? I'm Mrs. Wentworth. I just flew in from Nice."

"He's in room 210, next floor up, down the hallway past the nurse's station."

Danielle walked to the elevator, pressed the UP button and waited. Minutes seemed like hours. Perspiration ran down the back of her neck. The elevator took her to the third floor opened to a reception area. She walked to the nurse's station. "Hello. I'm Danielle Wentworth. I'm here to see my husband."

The nurse in blue scrubs smiled. "Let me see if he's able to have visitors."

"Yes, he should be fine. He had surgery this morning and may be groggy and is on pain meds." She pointed with her finger, "That way down the hall to room 210."

Danielle nearly sprinted down the hallway to his room. She bit her upper lip to keep from releasing a flood of tears. She brushed past the curtain and patient closest to the door to Evan's bed. He was hooked up to liquids, resting peacefully with his eyes closed. She quietly pulled up a chair and sat down, prepared for a long wait if necessary. He looked banged up, and sunburnt, which she expected. His forehead had stitches; his arms were full of yellow and deep purple bruises. She imagined his torso was full of gashes she could not see through the hospital gown. Evan's leg was in cast elevated on a bank of pillows. It seemed impossible that he was alive. Happy tears filled her eyes—tears of gratitude and relief. She nestled into the chair and closed her eyes, prayed and drifted off to sleep.

A doctor tapped Danielle on the shoulder. "Excuse me? Are you Mrs. Wentworth?"

"Yes. Oh, doctor. I'm sorry I fell asleep. I didn't want to wake my husband. Is he going to be okay?"

"Oh, yes, most certainly. We repaired his femur with a plate fixation."

"What's a plate fixation? When will he be able to walk?" Danielle wondered as she looked up at the portly doctor's smile, his round pleasing features and easy-going manner.

"By affixing a plate around the femur bone, it's then wrapped with wires that eventually meld into the bone. He will be able to walk with crutches, but it will take six weeks to regain 50% of the bone strength, and three months to get to 80%. He will have to be careful when moving around not to put full weight on the leg until the fracture heals."

Danielle nodded. "Then he didn't break his left leg?"

"It was a pretty severe spiral fracture, however, once it stabilizes and heals, he should be able to return to normal life."

"Will he be able to run? He likes to jog."

"Yes, I expect so. However, I would like to see him walking long distances first until the bone has completely healed. No jogging for a year. He's young, so that's in his favor."

"Are you the attending physician who did the surgery?"

"Yes, I'm sorry I didn't introduce myself. I'm Doctor Murphy. Brian Murphy."

"Happy to meet you. I'm Danielle. He seems to be sleeping so soundly, I didn't want to wake him up. Thank you for all you did for him."

Doctor Murphy shook Danielle's hand. "I'll be back later tonight to check on him. I expect he will be hungry since he survived on practically nothing for days."

"My father said he learned that Evan only had some avocados to sustain him. Seems like a miracle to me."

"It wasn't his time to die. He's going to be just fine. He's just groggy from pain meds and anesthesia."

Danielle smiled and nestled comfortably back into the chair watching Evan breathe—the best thing she had ever seen, her husband breathing life in and out.

"Hey sleepyhead."

Danielle's eyes opened wide and saw Evan staring at her. She lept up from her chair, put her arms around Evan and kissed him tenderly. "How do you feel?" she asked Evan.

"Sore, groggy, but famished. Do you know if they brought lunch yet?"

"No, but I'll check. I think it's time for dinner. You were sleeping so soundly I didn't want to wake you."

Evan adjusted the pillow behind his head. "Where are you staying?"

"At the *Calatrava,* in our room. If you can believe it, the hotel reduced the bill substantially because of your accident. They understood why you didn't return to the room. I am so impressed with their sensitivity and compassion."

"I need some compassion," Evan said. "Come here and let me kiss you again."

Danielle gave Evan a lingering, intense kiss. "I could do this all night. The fact that you're alive is unbelievable. You have to tell me what happened. I have so many questions if you feel up to it. How did you end up on the mountain?"

Evan sighed and shifted his shoulders. "Where do I begin?"

"You were going to book a flight home. What happened?"

"I got a phone call from the police. An officer recognized the photos I took from the pictures I left at the station. They told me they had seen Nick Fontaine at his boat on the wharf when that guy was murdered."

Danielle winced and gave Evan a conflicted look. "What guy?"

"Oh, sorry. The boatmate of Nick's was a guy named Chad Callahan. He was murdered. When the police came to investigate, they interviewed Nick. Apparently, he had words with Chad—something about the noise Chad made late at night on his boat."

Danielle gave Evan a quizzical glance. "What does that have to do with you?"

"Nothing. But once I knew what Ryan's name was here in Mallorca, Nick Fontaine, and where his boat was, I had to go there."

Danielle looked down at her feet and shook her head. "What did you plan to do if you found Ryan at his boat?"

"Stupid of me, but I couldn't arrest him—I'm no longer a cop and that was what was so frustrating; I think I wanted to beat the crap out of him, both for Ashley's sake and your father's controller, Armond. I went to the boat. I saw him on the deck with a woman. I started running toward the boat—he saw me and took off on his motorcycle. Without thinking I ran back to the car, and followed him."

Danielle twisted her lips and tilted her head. "Where did you think he was going?"

"I didn't think. I was filled with so much emotion and adrenalin, I just followed him. It became a car chase. I'm sure I put a few drivers in danger, and I'm responsible for Ryan's death."

"Why do you say that? You didn't kill him—you said he was run over by a truck."

"Yes, but if I hadn't been chasing him, he would have gone on living on this island as Nick Fontaine."

"What happened that you ended up in a car crash?"

"Ryan twisted over his shoulder during the car chase and fired his gun at me. He pulled out of the traffic lane and didn't seen a truck coming from the opposite direction. He was hit full on—probably was killed instantly. My mouth feels like cotton. Could you get me the water there with the straw?"

Danielle reached for the water container and handed it to Evan.

"Then what happened?" Danielle sat back down in the chair.

"I could see the truck heading toward me. It was going to topple over. I turned the car to the left to avoid the truck and could see the cliff coming. I opened the car door and fell out. The car went over the cliff and blew up upon impact. I clung to tree roots until they gave way sending me down the embankment. I plummeted down head over heels and ended up in the sand at the bottom of a cove."

Danielle's eyes were flooded with tears and she used the tips of her fingers to wipe them away. She was momentarily stunned by a knock at the door. "Oh, Dad. I'm so glad you're here." Danielle rose to greet her father with a warm hug.

Gaspard hugged Danielle, then reached over to shake Evan's hand. "How you doing?"

"I'm good—more than good. A little groggy and buzzed from the pain meds. Danielle's here and you're here. I want to thank you for rescuing me. Stuck in that cove in the sand was not how I wanted to die—in fact, I didn't want to die and I couldn't walk. I was pretty sure my leg was broken. Didn't see any boats or helicopters until you showed up."

"Excuse me," the attendant said. "Here's dinner."

Gaspard moved out of the way.

"What's for dinner?" Evan asked with raised eyebrows and wide eyes.

"Soup and saltine crackers, raspberry jello for dessert."

Evan wrinkled his nose. "Bummer. I want a hamburger, French fries—make that two hamburgers, and ice cream."

The attendant shook her head. "Tomorrow you can order from the menu, but the night after surgery, your stomach is not ready for such heavy food."

"I think we've stayed long enough, Danielle said. "After you eat, you need to rest. Dad, will you take me back to the hotel? You're staying at the *Calatrava*, right?"

"Yes. I booked a room. I'll leave in the morning. Are you planning to come home as well?"

Danielle frowned and brushed her auburn tresses off her face. "I think I'll stay another day. When Evan's stable, do you think he could be transported to the hospital in Nice so that he could recover there?"

"I'm sure. The Air Ambulance service here in Mallorca said they could transport him for a hefty fee, but they do this quite often when someone is ill here, recovers but is not able to fly. With Evan's leg, he probably can't be transported for several days. We'll have to ask the doctor. If Evan can be transported home, Chloe can take care of him at the hospital."

"I'm tired, Dad. Let's go back to the hotel, have dinner and get some sleep. I'll come back in the morning and hopefully talk to Dr. Murphy about how long Evan needs to be here before he could be transported safely."

Gaspard nodded. "Sounds good."

Danielle got up, leaned over Evan, kissed him on the forehead. "Enjoy that delicious dinner. I'll see you tomorrow."

"Oh, I forgot to mention. Some reporters with a camera were here earlier. They wanted to know how I survived the accident. I'll probably be on the news tonight."

Danielle smiled. "Best news ever."

CHAPTER 52
Cassie

Cassie finished packing up her clothing, wiped down the kitchen counters, tossed out food from the refrigerator, made the beds and swept the floors. Since the sailboat would be put up for auction, she wanted it as clean as possible given that she spent time there. Hoping not to run into obnoxious Mrs. Delmonico, she locked the doors, kept her head down and headed to her car. It was windy with a grey overcast sky that felt like rain. She drove to the police station, parked the car and went inside. "I'm Cassie Benoit. Is Officer Lopez here?"

The desk attendant rang Officer Lopez's phone. "There's a Cassie Benoit here to see you. Have a seat Ms. Benoit. He'll be out in a few minutes."

Cassie sat down and fidgeted with the keys looped around her fingers and glanced around the waiting room. Policemen entered the station, ignored her and went about their business.

"Ms. Benoit? Nice to see you again" Officer Lopez said while extending his hand to greet her. "What can I do for you."

"I wanted to bring the sailboat keys to you. It was a lot of work, but I cleaned up the boat so you can put it on the market."

Officer Lopez reached for the keys. "That was very helpful and will save us doing the work ourselves. By the way, did you see the newscast last night?"

Cassie curled her hair behind her ear. "No, I was busy cleaning. Why?"

"The man whose car went off the cliff survived the accident. They rescued him by helicopter. He's in the hospital here in Palma. His name is Evan Wentworth. I met him a few days ago when he was trying to locate Nick. I'm the one who gave him Nick's boat location."

Cassie frowned. "Do you know why Evan wanted to locate Nick?"

"I do, but I think it would be better if you went to see Evan and ask him yourself."

"I'll do that. I'm trying to get on with my life, but I have so many unanswered questions about Nick."

"I hope you find what you're looking for."

Cassie handed the keys to Officer Lopez. "So, do I." she exclaimed, turned and walked out of the police station.

Cassie drove to the hospital wondering what she would learn from Evan Wentworth, and whether it would bring any closure to her about Nick Fontaine. If Evan was the man who chased Nick down the dock to his motorcycle, she knew it had to be for a reason.

As she walked the halls of the hospital, she took a deep breath before reaching Evan's room. What would she say to him? Would he tell her the truth about why he had chased Nick—the chase that ended in Nick's death? She didn't expect anyone else to be in the room, but instead saw the back of a woman sitting in a chair.

"Hello. I'm Cassie Benoit. I wondered if I could talk to you about Nick Fontaine?"

Danielle stood. "I'm Evan's wife, Danielle Wentworth."

Cassie felt her hands get clammy, and did not extend hers. "I'm sorry to bother you. It's incredible you survived the accident. Were you the one who chased Nick up the Tramuntana? I was just talking with Officer Lopez and he said you could tell me why you were after Nick."

"Are you related to Nick?" Evan asked.

"No, not related. Nick was my construction foreman. I've built the new hotel *Cielo* which should open in another month. Where do you know Nick from?"

Evan motioned to the chair. "It's a long story. Why don't you have a seat."

"Nick had another name when he was the co-owner with my father-in-law, Gaspard DuBois, of Gaspard Yachting in Nice. He went by Ryan Coltrane. This isn't going to be easy for you to hear, and I'm sorry if this will be disturbing."

Cassie nodded, "Please continue."

"Ryan was caught embezzling and running drugs. Rather than face an embezzling charge, Ryan killed the company controller, Armond Fouquet, then later abducted my wife's sister, Lena. He blew up his yacht to fake his death."

Cassie leaned forward in her chair. "This is really difficult to hear."

"I can imagine it is, but there's so much more to the story. Prior to Ryan's coming to Nice, he and his brother orchestrated a bank robbery in Northern California. The robbery ended in gunshots killing several people including my six-year old sister, Ashley. Ryan Coltrane was an alias. His real name was Jed Reddiger."

Cassie bit her upper lip. "And you know all of this, how?"

"I used to be a detective. I've retired from the police force now, but when my wife accidentally saw Ryan working at your hotel site, we knew for sure Ryan had not died in the yacht explosion."

Cassie felt her skin pale, as if the blood were running from her head out of her toes. "It's so hard to believe. Nick was a very good worker and the crew really liked working for him. I was shot earlier this month—another long story which I won't go into, but Nick did everything he could to keep me safe. He was very good to me. It's hard to believe he was a killer with these past lives."

Evan asked Danielle to raise his bed. "He could be very charming, I'm sure, but he had a dreadful dark side."

Cassie stared blankly at Evan and Danielle. "A woman called me some weeks ago saying that Nick was Ryan something, I can't remember exactly. I thought she was mistaken, crazy or something. Was that you, Danielle?"

"Yes. Evan and I were on our belated honeymoon here in Mallorca. We took a drive up to your hotel's construction site, and I spotted Ryan. Sorry to keep using that name, but it's the name he used while working for my father. Although my husband always suspected that he faked his death, I had prayed he had died that day. When I saw Ryan, I wasn't sure it was him, if it was, I knew what it would mean to my husband. He put his own life in danger trying to rescue my sister, Lena who was left in a life raft by Ryan on the sea."

"Was your sister alive?" Cassie asked.

"Yes, she survived, but was traumatized for some time from the experience of being captured, drugged and nearly drowning."

"I see you have a cast on your leg," Cassie said.

"Fractured leg from the fall down the mountain."

"It's a miracle he's alive," Danielle said.

"This is all very hard for me to hear—it's not what I expected. I don't know what I thought, but certainly nothing this sinister. I had checked his resume after I hired him and it showed him as a co-owner of a housing construction company with his father. How does one spin a web of deceit so complex?"

"Ryan was very smart—covered his tracks really well. It took a long time for me to figure out who he really was."

"How did you learn who he was, what did you say, Jed Reddiger?"

"I contacted a yachting company in Southern California where Ryan said he worked, and it turned out he'd left that company in a hurry. It's another very long story, but he and his brother, Ted, were responsible for my sister's death."

"I'm devastated to have been so duped, and I'm sorry for your sister's death," Cassie added while folding her hands nervously on her lap.

"I feel responsible for his death," Evan said. "However, I now have justice for my sister—she was only six years old at the time. It's haunted me and now I have closure."

"Evan, tell Cassie about the gun," Danielle said.

Cassie met Evan's gaze. "What about the gun?"

"Just before the fatal accident, Nick, let's call him that, turned on his motorcycle and fired his gun at me. It shattered the window with a bullet hole. He would have killed me if he could. With me dead, he would have been able to go on living as Nick Fontaine."

Cassie rubbed her forehead. "I appreciate your taking the time to tell me all of this. I hope your leg heals, and that you will be going home soon."

Evan wiggled his toes sticking out of his cast. "I do too."

Cassie picked up her purse, stood and shook Danielle's hand and then Evan's. "I wish you both the best. Mallorca is a beautiful island. I hope you will have a chance to see it under better circumstances."

Evan and Danielle watched Cassie leave.

CHAPTER 53
Cassie

Cassie went to her car, opened the door, sat down and felt numb with grief mixed with anger. How could Nick have fooled her so convincingly? The Nick she knew was nothing like Ryan or Jed, his other aliases. She wondered if she saw what she wanted to see, oblivious to his dark side, but there was nothing he did to give her any hint of his past.

She reflected on their conversations on his boat—he lied to her with such ease, such confidence and convincing dialog that she saw no reason not to believe him. Perhaps he told her some truths—maybe he wanted to become something he wasn't in his past. She had slept with a killer which made her skin crawl. Tears welled up in her eyes—tears of guilt, anger and sorrow all mixed together in a confusing emotional torrent. She let them flow.

When her tears stopped, her head stuffed up from crying, she relaxed her shoulders and pondered her life. Nick had been nothing but helpful, conscientious, and kind to her. Perhaps he had a good side, or wanted to be a different person. Is one person all good or all bad? Certainly not. Learning about Nick's past, although exceptionally difficult to hear, gave her some closure. It would be far easier for her to forget Nick and not hurt so much from losing him. This was a story she would tell her father, Roberto, who would hold her close and tell her everything would be okay. She had a hotel to open, and grateful for her father's insistence to help her, life would go on. Cassie knew her heart would heal, but she would be more cautious in the future not to be hoodwinked by someone the way Nick had lied to her.

She started her car, shifted it into gear and drove to her apartment to pick up the pieces of her fractured life.

CHAPTER 54
Evan and Danielle

Nine Months Later

Evan and Danielle walked along the beach enjoying the abundance of floral fragrances, the salty sea breezes and the beautiful soft pinks, coral and yellow architecture of Nice. Although hardly noticeable, Evan walked with a slight limp. They held hands with Trevor who gingerly put one foot in front of the other. Danielle patted her bulging stomach and smiled at Evan. I hope this will be a girl, if that's all right with you.

"A healthy boy or girl is all I want," Evan stopped and placed his arm around Danielle's shoulders.

"My mother is planning a baby shower—she's so excited about having another baby to dote on."

"She loves to fuss, but your Dad is the one who takes the cake for being a doting grandfather."

"The kids in my 3rd grade class loved your "Let's Draw" program. Teaching children to appreciate art has added so much to their knowledge," Danielle said while kicking some sand out of her sandal.

"Do you think we'll take another really belated honeymoon, the one we didn't have because of the disaster in Mallorca? I was wondering where you might want to go next year after the baby is born?"

Danielle pondered the question. "Maybe the Grand Canyon would be interesting. Some place safe and exciting—something different from St. Paul-de-Vence and certainly not Mallorca, which I didn't get to see, but have no desire to revisit—too many painful memories."

Evan looked at Danielle. "The Grand Canyon would be very different. Where did you read about going there?"

"I was scrolling the Internet looking for spectacular places in the United States we hadn't seen. Knowing your parents would love to babysit, I thought we could visit them, leave the kids for a week or so, and enjoy ourselves."

Evan said, "I enjoy every day with you, and intend to do that the rest of our lives." He leaned over to give Danielle a kiss—a lingering embrace until Trevor shook them free, making giggling noises and pulling on both of his arms to keep walking.

THE END

Author Bio

Sherry Joyce, and award-winning author, writes Romantic Suspense and lives with her husband and two West Highland Terriers in Palm Desert, California. DANGEROUS JUSTICE is her third novel and the sequel to DANGEROUS DUPLICITY. She is an award-winning author who also wrote THE DORDOGNE DECEPTION. Her short story, COZUMEL CALAMITY has been published in OUR DANCE WITH WORDS, a collection of Fine Writing by Northern California Publishers and Authors; MURDER BY CONCLUSION was published by Sisters in Crime's 2016 Capitol Crimes Anthology.

If you enjoyed this novel, I'd love to hear from you. You can write a review on Amazon. Search books, enter DANGEROUS JUSTICE, and you will see a tab to write a review. Also, if you are interested, you might enjoy the prequel to DANGEROUS JUSTICE, DANGEROUS DUPLICITY.

ACKNOWLEDGMENTS

To my writing critique partners, Eileen, Carol, Joanne and Rocci, thank you for your valuable contributions and encouragement which made this book come to life in a better way. To my cover designer and fantastic webmaster, Rhonda Spring; Rob Preece with this tremendous formatting knowledge and skills. Once again, my husband, Jim, who supports my writing efforts by leaving me alone in the office for hours, and when reading the manuscript, always asking the right questions. To my dear friend and editor, Afton Tuveson, for her insight and eagle eyes for better writing.

Many authors write romantic suspense where robberies, murders and unpleasant things occur. However, those of us who believe in justice focus on the importance of solving crimes and preventing them. Grief, no matter what the reason, is difficult to deal with and can cause unsettled feelings long after the loss. The search for justice to overcome grief can take years or a lifetime before being able to move forward. This book was written for those who have experienced grief and understand the search for justice and the truth.

Made in the USA
Middletown, DE
01 June 2023

31884150R00130